To Kill a Witch

TO KILL A WITCH

Bill Knox

Constable • London

Constable & Robinson Ltd
3 The Lanchesters
162 Fulham Palace Road
London W6 9ER
www.constablerobinson.com

First published in Great Britain 1971
This edition published in Great Britain by Constable,
an imprint of Constable & Robinson Ltd 2006

A copy of the British Library Cataloguing in Publication
Data is available from the British Library.

ISBN 13: 978-1-84529-426-7
ISBN 10: 1-84529-426-2

Printed and bound in the EU

Chapter One

An imaginary boundary line runs down the exact middle of the River Clyde, a boundary that matters to the police divisions of the City of Glasgow. Dependent on which side of the line a body surfaces is the decision who'll own it in terms of trouble. Unless it looks like being swept straight down river to the sea. Then it automatically becomes Central Division's worry. They operate the launch patrols.

This one was decidedly Millside Division's property; had been from the moment it swirled into sight, half-submerged in the dirty grey water near the old King Street ferry steps. Gloomily, boat-hook ready, a uniformed constable stood on the lowest exposed step and tried hard not to get his feet wet. He glanced at his watch. It was 11.15 a.m., an otherwise pleasant, sunny Tuesday morning in early September, and he was going to miss his coffee break.

On top of which, he didn't like floaters. At best they came out like so much cold, wet putty. If they hadn't been mangled by some ship's propeller or been in so long they'd become bloated, stinking obscenities you couldn't wash out of your memory for days.

The body bobbed nearer. A woman, young, fair-haired, with a red cotton dress under what had been a short white raincoat. Both were now almost black with oily river scum. And, he noted idly, she'd had good legs.

Reaching out, the constable managed to snag the raincoat with the tip of the boat-hook and eased her nearer. The mortuary wagon was waiting, the crew of one of the divisional patrol cars were somewhere up on the quayside making noises about holding back spectators.

In other words, leaving him to get on with it. He changed position to improve his grip, felt cold river water pour into his left boot, but hardly noticed it.

The body had swirled round. There was a dark cord knotted round the throat. A narrow cord, tied so tightly that it was almost buried in the white flesh.

He cursed again as he shortened the boat-hook and dragged her in. It would be a C.I.D. job now, not a uniform branch worry.

But even so, why the hell couldn't she have gone to the south bank of the river, to Govan Division?

Chief Inspector Colin Thane, head of Millside Division C.I.D., felt pretty much the same when he received word. Particularly as he was at police headquarters in St Andrew's Square, one of the regular line-up of divisional chiefs assembled for the weekly crime conference.

The rumbling voice of Chief Superintendent Ilford, the large, bear-like boss of the city's detective force, had been giving the old familiar lecture about the need for a faster clear-up rate in divisional cases. But Ilford stopped as the conference-room door opened. Nine pairs of eyes watched warily as an orderly came towards the table with a slip of paper in one hand.

The note was laid in front of Thane. He read it quickly, conscious of the continued silence around. As he finished, he winced. The tooth which had begun aching at breakfast had come to life again. Maybe in sympathy.

6

'Well?' demanded Buddha Ilford from the top of the table. 'Trouble?'

Nodding, Thane eased back his chair. 'A floater, sir. But strangled first – they've just fished her out on our side of the river.' Across the table he saw a mixture of relief and commiseration cross the face of his opposite number from Govan Division. He grimaced slightly in that direction, then added, 'I'd better get on to it, sir.'

Ilford grunted agreement. 'All right. But keep in touch and try to wrap it up fast. That's advice for all of you, whatever the case – we've a crime graph that's beginning to look like the cost of living index.'

Thane left, closing the conference-room door behind him as the rumbling voice got under way again. Stopping in the corridor, he glanced again at the scribbled note. The message was from the Millside duty officer, a stark thirty-word rundown, ending with the fact that the body had been delivered to the city mortuary.

Which was a couple of minutes' walk from headquarters and he could rely on the division coping with early routine details. Mind made up, he ignored the elevator and took the stairway down to ground level. A couple of headquarters men grinned a greeting as he headed along the corridor to the main door. Thane nodded briefly, the tooth stabbing again, a corner of his mind wondering when he could find time to visit a dentist.

Then he was out in the open, heading down the busy, tenement-lined Saltmarket towards the red-brick mortuary building near its riverside end.

When it came to site locations, Glasgow was a practical place.

As he walked, several people recognized Thane's tall figure and long-legged stride. Most were neds, the city's verbal shorthand for petty thugs, second-rate criminals and professional layabouts.

For a start, Thane looked like a cop. In his early forties, wearing a softly checked blue gaberdine suit, he topped the six foot mark. Burly, with close-clipped dark hair and a tanned face usually politely classed as rugged, he moved with the muscular ease of a trained athlete. Years back, when he'd been a young beat constable and had carried a few pounds less weight, he'd been a more enthusiastic than successful amateur boxer in the heavyweight class.

Part of the rest, the part the neds didn't know, was that he was married with two children and a bunga-low home which had half the mortgage payments still to run.

What they could add, however, was that Colin Thane ranked as the youngest divisional chief in the city – and one of the most successful. Perhaps because he didn't worry too much about occasionally bending the rules. Or about kicking someone's backside if it would help things along.

So they moved till he'd passed, sliding into the nearest bar or bookie shop. Or, if they couldn't, gave a grudging nod then spat in the gutter once it was safe.

Things were friendlier at the mortuary. He found Doc Williams, the senior police surgeon, standing in the hallway finishing a cigarette.

'How was the conference?' grinned Williams, a lanky individual in an immaculately tailored dark business suit. 'I heard Buddha Ilford wasn't going to be in too happy a mood.'

'And this didn't improve it,' countered Thane dryly. 'Where is she, Doc?'

'In the side-room.' The police surgeon tossed the

rest of his cigarette into a sand-bucket, flicked a trace of ash from his lapel, then led the way down the cream-painted corridor. 'We've only had time to clean her up a little. But I've a notion the autopsy should be interesting.'

'I'm glad for you,' said Thane gloomily, following. Beneath the protective humour he knew Doc Williams was a professional. When the police surgeon said anything might be 'interesting' it meant the opposite of straightforward.

They reached the side-room and went in. The body was on a metal table in the middle, covered by a sheet. Two men were already in the room, a white-coated attendant and a Millside detective constable named Campbell. As they entered, Campbell looked relieved and took a step forward.

Thane greeted him with a nod and got straight to what mattered.

'What do we know about her?'

'Probable identity, sir.' D.C. Campbell always spoke as if he was already in the witness box. 'A purse was found in her coat pocket. It contained keys and a couple of credit cards, the cards made out in the name Margaret Barclay.'

'Who's checking?'

'Detective Inspector Moss, sir.' Campbell frowned a little. 'He said – ah – he'd better do the damned job himself.'

Thane fought down a grin, imagining how Phil Moss, his second-in-command at Millside, would curse that particular task.

'Better tell him the address, Campbell,' said Doc Williams mildly. 'Make his day.'

Campbell shrugged. 'Chelor Grove – out in Monkswalk.'

'So she's yours all the way,' mused the police surgeon. 'Correct?'

9

Thane grunted. Monkswalk was Millside Division's high-amenity suburban fringe. Monkswalk residents lived in an atmosphere of broad lawns, charge accounts, and au pair girls. They regarded a police force as an unfortunately necessary burden on the city's rates, a force necessary to keep the lesser elements of the population suitably subdued.

A floater from Monkswalk was trouble enough. A murdered floater would cause indignant uproar. His tooth began aching again, and this time he decided to blame the mortuary's low, air-conditioned temperature.

Doc Williams signalled. The attendant came over, drew back the sheet, and stepped aside.

They'd removed the woman's river-soiled clothing. Her legs were still marked by oily scum but the rest of her body lay white, naked and pitifully exposed under the neon-tube lights. One long strand of dark green bottom weed still clung to her short, fair hair.

'Natural blonde, you'll note,' said Doc Williams in a suddenly crisp, professional voice. 'From appearance, in the river about a week. That's about normal before they float at this time of year. Cause of death, strangulation by ligature.' He crossed over to a smaller table and returned with what had once been a pair of nylon panty-hose tights. They were still knotted together at the legs but had been cut loose above one knee.

'These?'

'Uh-huh.' He stretched the damp nylon experimentally. 'Speaking provisionally, she was attacked from the rear. The knot was at the back of the neck and whoever did it used plenty of strength. I had to almost dig this out.' He anticipated Thane's next question. 'She wasn't wearing stockings when we got her.'

'Sexual assault?'

10

'No obvious signs, but I'll let you know.'

'Right.' Thane looked again at the corpse. He guessed the woman had been in her late twenties. The eyes were blue, the nose a little too long to match the rest of her features, and the mouth was wide. But she'd been reasonably good-looking. He glanced at her hands. 'What about jewellery?'

Clearing his throat, D.C. Campbell answered from the background. 'No wedding ring, sir. But there was a fairly expensive-looking brooch on her dress, sapphires, in a gold setting. And about twenty pounds in the purse. Everything went over to Scientific Branch. I've got a list.'

'So you can probably strike out robbery,' mused Doc Williams. 'Maybe some boyfriend lost his grip, of course. But here's my little puzzle. Look at her forehead. Close up.'

Thane bent nearer, the smell of disinfectant not completely masking the other odour present.

'This.' Doc Williams traced a fingertip along the line of a narrow cut above the woman's eyebrows. It ran horizontally for about three inches, as straight and level as a rule. 'What do you make of it?'

'You tell me,' invited Thane cautiously.

'That's the only other sign of violence on her body and it didn't happen in the river. It's too fine a cut for casual contact – in fact, it's almost as neat as a surgical incision.' Doc Williams pursed his lips then made up his mind and finished. 'I think she was razor-slashed.'

'One cut, across the forehead?' Thane didn't hide his doubts. When a woman was slashed the result was usually in the multiple wound category, aimed at scarring for life.

'A razor or something as sharp,' said the police surgeon stubbornly. 'The wound could have been inflicted before or after death – I'll try to sort that out at the P.M.'

11

Thane stared at the cut again. 'You're suggesting a nut case.'

'Maybe, maybe not. There's something niggling in my mind about a wound like that.' Bleakly Doc Williams signalled the attendant, waited till the sheet had been replaced, then relaxed and glanced at his watch. 'Time for lunch. I'll start on her as soon as I get back. Feel like eating?'

Thane shook his head. 'I'll head for Monkswalk and see how Phil Moss is making out.' He turned to Campbell. 'Check with Criminal Records, see if the name Margaret Barclay means anything to them, then tell the fingerprint boys I want them here.'

After a week in water the task of taking prints from a body wasn't easy. The top layer of epidermal skin on the fingertips was always an early loss. But that still left the exposed dermis skin underneath and paraffin wax injections could counter the river's softening of tissues.

Whether he'd need fingerprints was for the future. The main thing was to get them. In fact, to gather any kind of evidence available and leave sorting out what mattered till later.

D.C. Campbell was heading towards the door. Thane made to follow him then stopped. 'Doc, do you happen to know a good dentist?'

'Meaning?' The police surgeon bristled indignantly. 'I can chart her teeth on my own. Look, if I had a penny for every time I've . . .'

'No, I meant for me,' said Thane wearily. 'Our regular man's on holiday.'

'That's different.' Doc Williams chuckled sympathetically. 'Well, there's no such animal as a painless dentist. But you're heading for Monkswalk. Jack Raddock is out there and he handles the fastest drill in town – or so he says. If it comes to an extraction he has a beautiful wrist-action. Sheer poetry to watch.'

Thane decided he'd wait. The ache might be gone by morning.

He looked again at the sheet-draped table. For a moment he wondered how the woman had been in life. How she'd walked, the way she'd laughed. Whether she'd been in love.

They'd have to start finding out. Among other things, that meant he'd have to phone home. Mary had a babysitter fixed, they'd planned a meal in town, then a cinema show somewhere. But any woman who married a cop – he let the thought end there, nodded to Doc Williams, and left.

A car from headquarters delivered Colin Thane to Monkswalk shortly after 1 a.m. Most of the way the radio had been muttering about an attempted bank hold-up in Eastern Division. But that might have been another world away as they cruised down a final, quiet, tree-lined avenue. The houses were individual, imposing, and uniform only in the way they spelled out money. So were the cars parked at the roadside, imported models that glinted in the sunlight and hadn't as much as a scratch on their paintwork.

'Makes you feel a flamin' peasant,' said his driver suddenly and gloomily. It was only the second time he'd spoken. The first had been a muttered blasphemy when they'd nearly rammed an errant pedestrian. 'How do you get into this league, sir?'

'First, you stop being a cop,' said Thane wryly. 'After that you're on your own.'

The driver grunted, unimpressed. Then he slowed the car. Chelor Grove was ahead, a compact, three-storey block of luxury apartments with a synthetic stone front, balconies, a private garage entrance and a sweep of garden which was a blaze of late-season rose bushes. A Millside Division car and one of the Scientific Bureau vans were parked outside, their uniformed drivers having a quiet smoke beside them.

Thane got out, thanked his driver, and watched the car start off on its return journey. Then, nodding to the uniformed men, he took the path through the rose garden towards the main door.

It was closed, with a security telephone grille beside its row of bell-pushes. Thane thumbed the button marked 'Barclay', waited, then heard a familiar grunt coming from the grille.

'Me, Phil,' he said briefly. 'Open up.'

'You took your time,' came the bitter reply. 'We're on the top floor.'

There was a click, the door swung open, and he went through into a tiled hallway. As he crossed to the elevator an apartment door to his left opened a fraction and he saw a woman peer out. Then just as quickly it closed again. Smiling a little, he took the car up, emerged in a carpeted corridor, and found a uniformed constable standing outside an apartment door.

'Natives friendly?' he asked mildly as the man saluted.

'Neutral, sir,' decided the constable. 'But bursting a gut with curiosity.'

Thane went into the apartment, then stopped and blinked. He was in the lounge, where the walls were painted a startling matt black with tangerine woodwork and a matt grey ceiling. The inner doors were faced with full-length mirrors, the carpet was wall-to-wall black, and furnishings amounted to little more than a couch and a couple of armchairs – inevitably in black again.

One of the mirror doors swung open, giving a glimpse of a bedroom. A scrawny, untidy figure in

14

a baggy tweed suit slouched out to meet him sardonically.

'Have a good lunch?'

'I had the chance. Doc Williams was buying.' Thane looked around the room again and grimaced. 'Is it all like this, Phil?'

'Mostly. Seems she was a freelance décor consultant, whatever the hell that means.' Detective Inspector Phil Moss, a small, grey man with thinning sandy hair, was in his mid-fifties and as usual looked as if he'd slept in his clothes. 'There's no sign of any kind of struggle, so it probably didn't happen here. But she's our floater for sure. Her keys opened the door, her description matches and the neighbours haven't seen her for over a week.'

Thane nodded. They'd need positive, formal identification, but it could wait. Another figure emerged from the bedroom, one of the Scientific Bureau technicians. He carried a small bag and a camera, murmured a greeting as he went past, and disappeared through another door.

'How about background?' Thane took out his cigarettes, lit one, saw Moss eyeing the pack hopefully, and passed them over.

'Thanks.' Moss helped himself, accepted a light, then admitted, 'There's not much that helps.'

'Today's surprise.' Thane sighed. 'Well?'

'She was Mrs Barclay – divorced, husband south somewhere. Age twenty-eight, lived alone, didn't get very much involved with the neighbours, and had a few men-friends around.'

'Any in particular?'

Moss shrugged. 'Played the field, according to the local oracle, Mrs Polson – she's on the ground floor, left.'

'We met, more or less.' Thane crossed to the bedroom, then stopped in the doorway, grinning. It was

15

a small room with a large bed, the décor switched to tangerine and black, and there was a balcony window. But what interested him was a pair of nylon-clad legs and plump bottom hunched almost under one side of the bed, the rest of their owner hidden from sight.

The bottom wriggled, there was a muttered curse, then the figure edged out into the open again, dragging a suitcase.

'Hello, Jean,' said Thane mildly. 'I thought it was you.'

Policewoman Cranston, a small brunette who now had a smear of dirt on her nose, smiled weakly as she rose and brushed fluff from her uniform.

'I – uh – brought her along because she's a woman,' said Moss weakly. 'I thought that might be useful.'

'Did you?' Thane winked at her and ignored Moss's splutter. 'Watch him, Jean. He's not dangerous. But too much excitement at his age . . .'

'Yes, sir, I know.' Jean Cranston had heard it all before, several times. She tried the suitcase, then frowned. 'This is locked.'

'Here.' Scowling, Moss tossed over a bunch of keys. 'One of them should do it.'

Thane stopped her, the humour gone from his voice. 'Jean, what do you reckon you know about Margaret Barclay so far?'

'From her things?' She chewed her lip slightly. 'Expensive taste in clothing and spent a lot on them. Fashion conscious too, but . . .' She paused.

'But what?'

'She hasn't been buying much lately. There's a coat and some skirts in the wardrobe that have been altered home-dressmaker style to bring them up to date.'

'Money running out?'

'It looks that way, sir. The same with make-up in her dressing table. Expensive perfume she's been using for a while but low-cost lipsticks and eye-shadow. You have to buy them more often.'

'Thanks, Jean.' Thane nodded appreciatively. Moss was a bachelor, Moss didn't know much about women except that they existed. So he'd done what, as far as he was concerned, was the obvious. As usual, it had paid off.

They left her and went back into the lounge. Stopping near the kitchen door, Thane frowned at a painting on the wall. It wasn't so much an explosion of colour as an obscure Technicolor spatter.

'I'd hate to live with this layout,' muttered Moss. 'It would give me ruddy nightmares.' He stubbed his cigarette, then stopped, his face twitching. In a moment he underlined his feelings with a monumental belch. As the sound died, he sighed in a mixture of relief and apology. 'I've been waiting for that one.'

Thane didn't comment. Phil Moss and his stomach ulcer were part of Millside Division folklore, if occasionally wearing. 'A magnificent duodenal' was how it had been tagged by one specialist dragged in as much to admire as treat it. Any notion of surgery was repelled by its owner. Moss preferred to nurse it along on a variety of hopeful remedies.

Mildly this time, Moss belched again. 'I put Sergeant MacLeod and young Beech on digging around her friends. Mrs Polson downstairs knew a couple of names.'

'And we'll have to check the ex-husband,' mused Thane. That was routine too. Family were top of the suspect list on the average murder investigation. He turned away from the picture. 'But there's another possibility, Phil. One I don't like. You heard how she was marked?'

'The cut across her head?' Moss nodded. 'It could mean a wandering odd-ball, I suppose. But maybe not.' He scraped a hand across his chin, rasping a patch of stubble he'd missed that morning. 'You'd better see the kitchen.'

Without explaining further he led the way. Two more Scientific Bureau men were in the kitchen. It was a small, bright room with the same shade of tangerine plus white, and well equipped.

'I meant to tell you.' Moss pointed towards the stainless-steel sink. Two used glasses stood on the draining board, already dusted with grey fingerprint powder. A single cup and saucer and a small mound of dirty dishes were still in the sink. 'She had company before she left.'

Bending over, Thane sniffed and could still catch a faint aroma of whisky from the glasses. He glanced at the nearest Bureau man, who'd been prodding through a waste bin.

'Two clear sets of prints on them, Chief Inspector,' confirmed the man.

'Any luck with the rest of the place?'

'Too early to say. We'll need to sort out what we've got.'

Which amounted to the standard Scientific Bureau reply. Thane sighed, nodded, and headed back into the lounge. Jean Cranston was there, an odd expression on her face, the opened suitcase lying on a chair beside her.

'Would you look at this, sir?' she said strangely. 'I – well, I don't know what to make of it.'

He went over, Moss at his heels. Then blinked.

The case held a strange assortment of unrelated items. Prodding with a finger he saw tangled lengths of wool and dried grasses, a necklace that seemed made out of bird claws, a pair of open-toed sandals, beads, and what looked like a piece of an old brass lamp. He took out a glass jar with a screw-top lid, opened it, and wrinkled his nose at the smell from its greasy contents.

'What the hell?' muttered Moss, staring at the rest.

'This was on top of it, sir.' Jean Cranston lifted a short black velvet cape from the arm of the chair and spread it out. The cape fastened at the neck by a single button.

Slowly, Thane replaced the jar then stared down at the rest, frowning. Then he took the cape, put it in with the rest, and closed the lid.

'Sir . . .'

The sound of a telephone ringing stopped Jean Cranston. Crossing over to a corner table, Moss lifted the receiver. He listened for a moment then glanced round.

'It's Beech, Colin. He's with a woman named Katherine Foulis – her husband's some kind of insurance executive and they live locally. She says Margaret Barclay was at a party she gave last Monday. She came late and left early with the same man.'

'Name?'

'Drew Tulley. Mrs Foulis doesn't know much about him.'

Crossing over, Thane took the receiver. Detective Constable Beech was young, brash, but no fool.

'Thane. How many were at the party, Beech?'

'About a dozen, sir.' Beech's voice crackled uneasily on the line. 'I'm – uh – with Mrs Foulis now.'

'So I won't ask awkward questions. But get their names, all of them. If she doesn't know much about Tulley, who invited him?'

'Hold on, sir.' He heard Beech mutter for a moment in the background and a woman's voice answer. Then

Beech was back on the line again. 'Mrs Foulis told Margaret Barclay to bring a friend, to keep the numbers even. But she has a feeling her husband might know more about Tulley.'

'Then get hold of the husband, find out, and check back with me before you do anything else,' ordered Thane. He hung up, felt his tooth nagging again, but had too much on his mind to worry about it. 'Phil, ask your Mrs Polson to come up here. I want to talk to her.'

'When she's around you don't talk, you listen,' warned Moss wryly.

'I'll risk it.' He watched Moss pad off towards the door, then turned to Jean Cranston with a touch of irritation. 'Didn't this Barclay woman keep a diary, an address book – or scribble phone numbers on the walls somewhere?'

'If she did I haven't found them yet, sir,' she answered calmly. 'But I haven't had time to look everywhere.'

'No – and the chances are somebody beat us to it.' Thane glanced down at the suitcase. 'Any notion why she'd hide that junk in a locked case?'

Policewoman Cranston fingered the top button on her tunic unhappily, then answered without any particular conviction.

'They could be souvenirs, sir.'

'Souvenirs of what?'

'Well, they're weird. But she might have been a hippy when she was younger – people change.' She looked round the room and added hastily: 'In some ways, anyway.'

'It's possible.' Thane kept his face expressionless. He had a strange feeling of his own about the collection. But it was one that could keep. Lifting the case, he dumped it in her hands. 'Put this back in the bedroom for now. And keep looking.'

Mrs Eunice Polson was plump and sixty, wore a lemon trouser suit which might have looked good on a teenager but only emphasized the spread of her hips, and had a blue-rinse hairdo. She came into the apartment on a waft of Chanel, smiled politely as Moss made the introductions, then glanced around with eager, bird-like eyes.

'Thanks for coming up,' said Thane, ignoring Phil Moss's flickering wink. 'I won't keep you long, Mrs Polson.'

'If there's any way I can help, I will,' she declared swiftly. 'When I think of that poor girl being murdered, how any of us could have been murdered . . .' She stopped and dropped her voice to a more confidential tone. 'How was she killed, Chief Inspector? Was she shot?'

'Strangled.'

The bird eyes glinted. 'Sex?'

Thane blinked. 'You think it might have been?'

She sniffed. 'Well, that's the usual reason, isn't it?'

'There can be others.' He waited till she'd settled in an armchair, then offered her a cigarette. She took one, and the hand which shielded the flame of his lighter glittered with two of the chunkiest diamond rings he'd seen. 'How well did you know Margaret Barclay?'

'Better than most people in this block, I suppose.' Mrs Polson looked around for an ashtray and waited till Moss brought one over. 'She was divorced – you'll know that, of course. I'm a widow. So we were both women living on their own. Different in age groups, though I believe you're only as old as you choose to be.' She paused, as if waiting for a comment. None

21

came, she looked slightly disappointed, and carried on. 'She was a bright girl, specially gifted, intelligent – we had a lot in common.'

'Did she talk much about herself?'

'No, not particularly.' Her eyes strayed as one of the Bureau men left the kitchen, crossed the lounge behind them, and entered the bathroom. As the bathroom door closed, she quivered slightly. 'Where was she killed, Chief Inspector? Was it here, in the apartment?'

'It doesn't look that way, but we've a lot to do before we're sure.' Thane saw her eyebrows rise as the bathroom toilet flushed noisily and took the chance to get another question in. 'How was she placed financially?'

Mrs Polson chilled a little. 'If one lives in Chelor Grove one obviously can maintain certain standards. And one doesn't pry.'

'No,' he soothed quickly. 'But without prying, just because you knew her, you would notice things. Things that might help. For instance, this interior decoration business she ran . . .'

'The décor consultancy?' Mrs Polson crossed her fat, trousered legs with care. 'I think it did quite well. Though – ah – perhaps not so much recently. She was at home more often during the day.'

'Did she have a car?'

'No.' The lemon shoulders shrugged delicately. 'But then she didn't really need one. She had plenty of friends to take her places.'

'Men?'

'Mostly, I suppose.' Mrs Polson tried to appear reluctant but leaned forward. 'Well, to be honest, between being on the ground floor and beside the elevator I sometimes couldn't help notice what was happening.'

'Of course not,' he agreed solemnly.

'After all, she was young, quite attractive, and one doesn't want to be too old-fashioned about that sort of thing – provided it doesn't become too obvious.'

'Meaning some of them stayed overnight?'

She nodded. 'Or she'd go off with a suitcase for a few days.'

'And that's what you thought had happened when she disappeared?'

'Yes, though I couldn't understand how . . .' Mrs Polson stopped quickly and corrected herself. 'What I mean is . . .'

Thane helped her out. 'Were you home last Monday evening, Mrs Polson?'

'No, I was at a show in town.' Understanding dawned. 'Was that when . . . ?'

He nodded. 'We'll ask you for a proper statement later, and descriptions of people you saw coming or going. But did Margaret Barclay ever talk about these men?'

'No. And I could hardly ask.'

The telephone rang. Thane waited till Moss answered. In the background the bedroom door opened and Jean Cranston looked out. He shook his head slightly and she quietly closed the door again.

After a moment Moss replaced the receiver. 'Head-quarters,' he reported laconically. 'About your C.R.O. query – they say there's no listing of a Margaret Barclay.'

'Right.' Thane considered Mrs Polson again, then asked quietly: 'What sort of person was she, Mrs Polson? Wouldn't you say there were other ways in which she was different from the ordinary?'

Something close to puzzlement crossed her face. The diamond-cluttered fingers went up to the throat of the high-necked silk blouse she wore beneath the suit jacket, their tips feeling for something beneath the fabric's smooth sheen.

23

'That depends on what you mean,' she said, almost reluctantly. Her fingers stayed at her throat. 'As I told you, Margaret was gifted and – and helpful.'

'Specially gifted, specially helpful?'

She moistened her lips. 'Yes. But you must know . . .'

Thane stopped her. 'You tell me, Mrs Polson. She helped you?'

'Yes.' She took a deep breath. 'Which was more than my doctor could.'

'I see.' He glanced at Moss, who raised an eyebrow but eased away from them, trying to appear interested in one of the pictures on the wall. 'What happened?'

'For years I had headaches, headaches which were getting worse all the time. Then I'd suddenly start weeping in the middle of the day – or I'd be out somewhere and feel I was going to faint. Pills didn't do any good. Then, about three months ago, I heard Margaret had helped someone else. So I asked her.' The fingers dipped deep into the neck of her blouse and came out with a necklet of crocheted red wool. A tiny pendant of metal dangled from its end. 'She gave me this and told me to wear it. I've been cured ever since.'

Thane drew a deep breath. 'Did she tell you why it would work?'

'Yes. But –' the bird-like eyes showed astonishment – 'but I thought you knew. She was a witch, Chief Inspector. Anyone in Chelor Grove could have told you!'

Chapter Two

It was 4 p.m. and starting to rain when the C.I.D. car returned to the Millside Division police office. Colin Thane got out, drew a deep breath, and for once blessed the solid reality of the building's grimy Gothic ugliness. Even the vandalized posters on the notice board and the broken bottle lying in the gutter near the main door seemed to extend a welcome.

'Finished with the car?' asked Moss, joining him.

He nodded, waved the driver on his way, and they went in through the main door. At the uniformed-branch public counter a woman with a black eye and a shopping bag was roasting the bar sergeant. She wanted her husband back. The fact that he'd been locked up the night before for giving her the black eye seemed immaterial.

The sergeant saw them and winked. Along a corridor the teleprinter chatter and background static of the communications room took over as they climbed the stairs to C.I.D. territory. The main office was almost deserted and by common consent they said nothing till they were in Thane's room with the door closed and the crime map on the wall – a final, pin-studded return to normality.

'Monkswalk's friendly neighbourhood witch.' Thane flopped into the battered leather armchair behind his desk and sighed. 'What the hell have we got ourselves into this time?'

'Trouble.' Slouched back against a filing cabinet, Moss grunted the word, belched, and fished a tiny bottle of pills from his pocket. He fed one into his mouth, swallowed, then went on as if there hadn't even been a pause. 'Just trouble like always, except this one's on a broomstick. What do we do next?'

'Keep digging – like always.' Absently, Thane flicked open the cardboard file in front of him. One glance at the pile of reports and paperwork waiting and he closed it hastily. 'At least we know the racket she was working.'

If racket was the word. He'd started a double-check after Mrs Polson's story of the necklet charm. So far the men out door-knocking had come up with five other instances of people near Chelor Grove who'd asked Margaret Barclay for various kinds of help. Monkswalk's witch hadn't charged for her services. Instead, she'd suggested a donation if the customer was satisfied. A donation of twenty pounds and four out of five had paid up.

'She wouldn't make a fortune at it,' said Moss warily. 'Thinking of a dissatisfied customer?'

'Not particularly – yet.' Thane grimaced. 'I'm more interested in what this character Drew Tulley will have to say.'

There, at least, they'd had some success thanks to D.C. Beech and his interview with Katherine Foulis's husband. Margaret Barclay's escort to the Monday party was a travelling salesman, still at work as usual and somewhere out in the city with his sample case. He was due back at base at four-thirty and Beech was waiting to bring him in.

'Tulley?' Moss was cynical. 'I can guess his story. He took the Barclay woman home, she waved good-bye, and he doesn't know a thing. What's more, we'll have a hell of a job proving otherwise.' Levering up from the filing cabinet, he blew his nose on an off-white handkerchief. 'I could talk to the uniformed branch and find out who they've usually got on the night beat around Chelor Grove. He should know something about what goes on in his patch, including any wandering witch.'

Thane wondered. He could think of some beat cops who if they saw a witch would probably try to book her for flying without lights. But he nodded.

'Do that. Then nudge the Scientific mob and tell them we need anything they've got. But do it gently – they're howling about being overworked.'

'And Buddha Ilford?' reminded Moss.

'Can wait.' Thane could hear the growl already. The city C.I.D. chief was going to love this kind of background. 'Two other things, Phil. When the rest of the stuff from her apartment arrives I want it brought in here. Meantime, check on this decorating consultancy thing she was running – what went wrong, anything else you can get.'

Moss nodded, reached the door, then glanced back. 'Fancy a sandwich? I could send out for something.'

'That's your best suggestion yet. And if the switchboard have a kettle boiling . . .'

'Right. The sandwiches – who pays?'

'Your turn.'

It brought a grunt, which he'd expected. Chuckling, Thane lit a cigarette as Moss went out. Then he glanced instinctively at the crime map. Two safe-blowings, a razor-slashing, yesterday's attempted hold-up, the man they'd caught molesting kids, the usual crop of thefts and robberies . . . each pin translated as it caught his eye.

They'd need another one now, for Chelor Grove. Cigarette dangling, he quit the chair and went over to the window. It was still raining and the street glinted wet below. Beyond it was raw, scarred earth which had been a block of rat-infested tenements till a month before. Then the demolition squads had moved in, slicing them open, hammering them down.

For a moment he remembered the tattered wall-papers suddenly exposed to daylight. The crazy irrelevance of a housewife's forgotten apron hanging on a hook behind a door with nothing below it but a three-storey drop. The neds who'd stolen anything salvageable from the ruins after dark – until the desk sergeant arrested six of them single-handed in one night. He'd complained it was the only way he could get peace to read the racing results.

Millside had most things. It was that kind of division, born in dockland, constituting an oblong slab of Glasgow's north-west. Which meant everything from bingo halls and bookies to Monkswalk and its status symbols. From teenage knife gangs to white-collar workers who embezzled to keep up their car payments.

Millside Division could be rough and tough or smooth and slippery. Headquarters kept its secrets, but Thane knew there had been arguments both ways before he had been given the division, transferred from the regional crime squad. With, as some unknown genius's contribution to the balance, Phil Moss slotted as his second-in-command from a Central Division desk job.

They were opposites in almost everything that could be named. But it worked, an odd amalgam of talents and temperament.

In a way, Phil Moss was the key. To be older yet junior was something he didn't resent. His small, slight build made it a legend that he'd either bribed or stood on tiptoe to get by the minimum height stipulation at the police entrance medical. Added to which he was complaining, insolent, and the despair of a landlady who had to battle to keep him from looking like a welfare case. But he was still the patient, sifting, assessing member of the team – the type who treated wandering into the middle of a back-street brawl as an annoying incidental.

Thane was different and knew it. Patience was something he fought daily to achieve and didn't always attain. While he'd enlist every kind of aid going, from scientific onward, he'd still throw every established conclusion aside and gamble on a hunch he believed to be right.

Usually he was lucky. But when things went wrong Phil Moss stepped in. Still complaining, sarcastically ignoring their difference in rank. But always ready with a fresh possibility which might rescue the situation.

This time? He wondered, still staring out at the rain, then turned as he heard a knock on the office door. It opened and an orderly came in balancing a mug of tea and a plate of sandwiches in one hand, Margaret Barclay's suitcase in the other. He dumped the suitcase on the floor, laid the mug and sandwiches on the desk, then cleared his throat cautiously.

'Sir . . .'

'Well?' Thane was already over and using a ball-point pen to stir the tea.

'The pay section phoned from headquarters while you were out. They – uh – still haven't had the C.I.D. overtime sheet for last week.'

'It's here somewhere.' Sighing, Thane rummaged through the neglected correspondence file, found the sheet, and used the ballpoint to scrawl his signature at the foot. In the process his hand bumped the mug and tea spattered across the inked figures. Swearing, he tried to wipe them clean – then swore again as a protruding pin ripped a deep gash across two of his fingers.

Blood smeared on top of the rest. He gave up, tossed the sheet to the determinedly straight-faced orderly, then slumped into his chair as the man went out. Blood, tea, and ink – that summed up the score when you held a Division job.

The sandwiches were salami and pickle. He'd finished one and was starting the next when the telephone began ringing. Taking a quick gulp from the mug, he picked up the receiver and prayed it wouldn't be Buddha Ilford.

'Thane . . .'

'MacLeod, sir,' crackled a gloomy voice on the line and he relaxed again. Detective Sergeant MacLeod was large, fat, and reliable. 'I'm still at Chelor Grove, and I thought you'd better know what's happened.'

'It always helps,' agreed Thane with a mild sarcasm. 'Do I guess or do you tell me?'

'Sorry.' MacLeod sounded hurt. 'I'm at the Barclay woman's apartment and we've just had visitors – a couple called Foulis. They had their lawyer with them and they're kicking up hell about the way they were quizzed by D.C. Beech. Something about a party the Barclay woman was at.'

'I know. Where are they now?'

'On their way to see you, by car. I wouldn't call them friendly, sir.'

'We'll cope – and thanks for the warning.' Thane hung up, grimaced, and could guess what was happening. At best, young Beech had all the tact of a runaway carthorse. But more important, Monkswalk householders went pale at the thought of getting involved in anything that didn't slot into the business or society columns.

The second sandwich finished, he drank the last of the tea, then cleared a space on his desk and opened the suitcase. Taking out a large envelope, he spilled the contents on the desk. Bankbooks and receipts, old letters, a passport, the bundle amounted to all

30

the personal papers they'd been able to gather in Margaret Barclay's apartment.

Reading through them systematically, he was lighting a fresh cigarette when the door swung open and Moss came in.

'Mind?' Moss helped himself from the pack and borrowed Thane's lighter, his watery blue eyes taking in the littered desk. 'Anything interesting in that lot?'

'Not much – and nothing on the witchcraft side. If somebody did search her flat, they made a darned good job of it.' Thane pointedly tucked his cigarettes away. 'Her bank balance was slipping fast, like we guessed. But there's a regular eighty pounds payment listed on the first of each month.'

'Alimony?'

'That's how it looks. We can trace the ex-husband through the cheque.'

'I'll organize it,' agreed Moss. 'But there's a chance the rest is going to be easier. Beech radioed in. Drew Tulley's office has closed for the night. Tulley didn't check in and they can't understand it. He certainly hasn't been home so . . .'

'So we'd better find him,' said Thane tightly. 'All right, Phil. Make this a special search request, all divisions.'

'I did,' reported Moss with an acid satisfaction. 'Description and car details, plus two plain-clothes men covering his apartment block. Beech is on his way back in.'

'Now?' Thane got up quickly, crossed to the door, and looked out. There were only two men left in the duty room, the nearest dictating a report into a spool recorder.

'Sam.' He waited till the recorder was switched off. 'Contact Beech. Tell him to stay away from here. Tell him to – to – hell, tell him to do anything you want.

But I don't want his face inside this station till I say so.'

The detective raised an expressive eyebrow but headed for the radio room.

'What's he done this time?' asked Moss resignedly.

'Maybe nothing.' Thane closed the door again. 'But Mrs Foulis and her husband are on their way here with a lawyer. I don't want Beech around to complicate things.'

The telephone rang. Grinning, Moss answered it, listened, and the grin slipped into a frown. He put a hand over the mouthpiece.

'It's started, Colin. The *Evening Bugle* news desk has a tip about a murder somewhere in Monkswalk. They're right on their last edition deadline. Can we confirm?'

Slowly, Thane shook his head.

'Never heard of it,' said Moss, and hung up. Then he scratched his chin thoughtfully. 'They'll love us for that later.'

'The mornings will have it – but official, through headquarters. Which wins us some time to know what the hell we're doing,' said Thane shortly.

Usually he co-operated with press and TV. News stories, even the critical kind, had a habit of bringing in witnesses and could help in a score of other ways. But he preferred to know at least a few of the answers before he started talking.

Moss shrugged. 'Well, I haven't much that's going to do us any good. The Scientific mob say all finger-prints at the apartment were Margaret Barclay's, except for a set on one of the whisky glasses. They've no previous record of her prints or the unidentified set.'

'That's all from them?'

'Except for mumbling noises,' said Moss caustically. 'But I got a little as far as her decorating agency is concerned. A few people in the business used her work till about a year ago. Then she began turning out non-stop gloom and occult signs and the customers just faded away.' He stubbed his cigarette. 'Last on the list, the beat cop for Chelor Grove is Danny Seaforth.'

Thane winced. 'Six feet thick and Highland?'

'That's the one. I said we'd contact him out there.'

The telephone rang again and this time Thane answered it.

'Tell them to wait,' he said after a moment and hung up.

'Foulis, Foulis, and lawyer?' queried Moss.

'At the front counter. Waiting won't harm them.' As he spoke, Thane began gathering up the papers on his desk. He stopped at a small, separately tied bundle he hadn't noticed before.

'Unopened mail we found behind her door,' explained Moss. 'I didn't have time to check it.'

There were about a dozen letters. Thane split the bundle, gave some to Moss, and they began opening the envelopes. Most were circulars or bills, but Moss suddenly chuckled and slid a card towards him.

'Raddock – isn't that the dentist Doc Williams told you about?'

'Uh-huh.' Thane glanced at the card.

J. A. Raddock, dental surgeon, regretted Mrs Barclay hadn't kept her last appointment. She should telephone and arrange a new date. Tongue automatically seeking the ragged cavity in his tooth, Thane turned the card over. The postmark was three days after Margaret Barclay had disappeared.

He set it aside, threw away a circular from a cut-price liquor store, then stopped at the last in his batch. It was a small envelope, faintly perfumed, the address handwritten, posted two days before. Inside was a single sheet of high-quality notepaper headed with a Monkswalk address. Thane read the letter and whistled softly.

'Phil . . .' He held it out.

Moss took the letter, twitched a nostril at the perfume, then muttered the short message aloud.

'Our new coven meets on Thursday. Join us then in Black Donald's name – Jane and Arthur Gibb.' Puzzled, he tapped the letter against the desk-top. 'Who's this character Black Donald?'

'If you were raised anywhere outside of a city, you'd know that one,' answered Thane softly. 'He's Auld Hornie, the Big Speckled Fellow, Nickie Ben – old man Satan himself.'

Moss grunted, unimpressed. 'I'm just a plain, old-fashioned, out-of-benefit Presbyterian. What's a coven? Some kind of fan club?'

'Near enough.' Carefully, Thane slid the letter back in its envelope. 'We'll talk to these people. But I'll get the Foulis business over first. Trundle them up.'

Lean, tall and middle-aged, Frank Foulis was the complete, successful businessman from his highly polished black shoes to his golf-club tie. He had a small dark beard and the spotless white handkerchief in his breast pocket looked as though it had been sewn in place. His wife, a plump brunette, had probably been an eye-catcher fifteen years before and dressed as if she remembered it.

They came into Thane's office with their lawyer hovering behind like a thin-faced guardian vulture. Thane recognized him. Ernie Cornfoot made an occasional appearance at criminal trials though his main income came from arguing with the Inland Revenue. A wary rearguard, Moss winked over their shoulders, then made the introductions. Cornfoot shook hands

34

limply, his clients contenting themselves with tight-lipped nods as they took the chairs Moss slid forward.

'I heard you were coming,' said Thane in a deceptively mild voice. 'What's the problem, Mr Cornfoot? I can't spare much time.'

'We appreciate that, with a murder on your hands.' Cornfoot gave a brief, professionally sympathetic smile which was weak at the edges. 'And, of course, Mr Foulis and his wife have already acted as responsible citizens in giving any help they can. But – ah . . .'

'They'd forgotten something?' suggested Moss innocently.

'No.' Cornfoot looked pained. 'Chief Inspector, they feel rather – ah – perturbed.'

'Why?' asked Thane, wooden-faced. 'There's no suggestion they're in any danger, if that's what's worrying them.'

'No, but one can overlook the –' Cornfoot hesitated uneasily – 'well, the personal difficulties.'

'Why tiptoe round it?' demanded Foulis, leaning forward, both hands on Thane's desk. 'We've told you what we know and now we want to be kept out of it. I'm in the insurance business, where you burn up if there's the wrong publicity. My wife's on so many damned charity committees she loses count. If some stupid bitch of a woman gets herself killed by a boyfriend that's not our fault.'

His wife nodded emphatic agreement. 'We want to help, of course. But there were other people at that party, business friends . . .'

'Contacts is the word,' growled Foulis. 'I don't want them dragged into it. Things are bad enough already. I don't like a detective barging into my office waving his warrant card and having me dragged out of the executive washroom.'

Thane fought off a twinkle. In the background Moss blew his nose loudly.

35

'So what's your suggestion?' asked Thane quietly.

'A reasonable one,' declared Cornfoot, eagerly determined to earn his keep. 'Full co-operation with the police, of course. Just – ah – well, surely it would be possible for the Crown case to go forward without any specific mention of what was a perfectly innocent gathering?' His voice sank to a hopeful purr. 'After all, Tulley can't deny he left the house with the Barclay woman.'

They sat silent, waiting, while Thane considered the ceiling for a moment. Suddenly he came back to them.

'Mrs Foulis, how well did you know Margaret Barclay?'

'More or less casually.' She reddened and waved a vague, emerald-ringed hand. 'We had mutual friends, she mixed well with people, talked brightly – people like that are always useful if you're giving a party.'

Her husband grunted through his beard. 'That's maybe out of your depth, Thane. But it's true.'

'She talked brightly,' mused Thane, unperturbed. 'You mean about being a witch?'

'That nonsense?' Foulis's eyes narrowed. 'Look, she could have said she was a bloody fairy in disguise for all I cared. What does it matter now?'

'Mrs Foulis?'

Her mouth opened and closed a couple of times. Cornfoot started to speak, but Thane stopped him with a glare, then swung open the suitcase lid. The black velvet cloak and the rest of Margaret Barclay's witchcraft collection lay under the light like so much debris.

'Ever seen any of these before?' he asked bluntly.

Foulis barely glanced then shook his head.

'Mrs Foulis?'

'No.' Her plump face was unhappy. 'I knew she believed in witchcraft, that's all.'

'She did.' Thane closed the lid again, his mouth

tightening. 'But it didn't stop her being strangled and dumped in the river.'

As Katherine Foulis winced, Cornfoot cleared his throat in a fresh protest.

'Chief Inspector, is this necessary?'

Ignoring him, Thane turned to Foulis again and eyed him icily. 'That's all for now. I'll want full statements from you and your wife. But get off my back, Foulis. And understand this – you're a witness whether you like it or not.' He sat back, deliberately folding his arms. 'A witness has a right to protection. We might decide that means a squad car parked outside your home twenty-four hours a day. Or a uniformed man being around to escort you to work.'

'That's a threat,' squeaked Cornfoot.

'Shut up,' said Foulis softly. He drew a deep breath, signalled his wife, and they got to their feet. For a moment the bearded face stayed angry then something close to a smile twisted across it. 'Message received and understood, Chief Inspector. If it's of any interest –' he glanced at his wife – 'this wasn't completely my idea.'

'No?' Thane paused, his face expressionless. 'One thing before you go, Mr Foulis. We need formal identification of the body – tomorrow morning would do. If you can spare the time.'

'Me?' Foulis swore under his breath but shrugged a bitter acceptance. 'All right, I know when I'm in a corner. Come on, Kate, we're leaving before they think of anything else.'

They went out, Cornfoot hurrying after them making apologetic noises.

'Come home, D.C. Beech, all is forgiven?' queried Moss with a dour satisfaction.

Thane nodded, then swore under his breath as the

thought connected with another. He still hadn't telephoned home and Mary would be getting ready to
meet him.

'Phil, I'll go out to the Gibbs' now. Get a car organ-
ized while I make a call – and I'll want you to watch
the shop till I get back.'

'If you get back,' grunted Moss. 'Maybe they'll turn
you into a plastic gnome, with king-sized feet.'

Once he'd gone, Thane lifted the telephone, got an
outside line, and dialled his home number. It was
Tommy who answered at the other end. His son had
a twelve-year-old's typical lack of diplomacy.

'If you're going to tell her you're working late, then
you're in trouble,' came his youthful treble over the
line. 'Mum's had her hair done, special. And Clyde's
been sick over the hall carpet.'

'Just get your mother,' said Thane wearily.

He waited, hearing Clyde barking somewhere in
the background. Sixty or so pounds of schizophrenic
boxer dog with a wrecking complex wasn't so much
a household pet as a liability, one he'd personally
have moved long ago. Except that the rest of the
family would probably have treated him like a leper
from that moment on.

'Sorry – I was zipping my dress.' Slightly breath-
less, still hopeful, Mary's voice came on the line.
'There's nothing wrong, is there?'

'Yes.' He drew a deep breath. 'Mary, I'm sorry, but
tonight's off. There's been a murder – a woman from
Monkswalk.'

'Oh.' It came flatly. 'When did it happen?'

'Last week. But we only found her late this afternoon.' He rounded off the minor lie in what he hoped
was convincing style. 'This is the first chance I've had
to call you. Look, we can make it Friday . . .'

'When your mother is coming to hold court?' Her
voice frosted.

'Well, I'll fix up something,' he promised hastily.

She sighed, then thawed a little. 'Back to tea and television with the kids. Will it be an all-night job?'

'Maybe.' The crisis over, he found a cigarette one-handed and lit it thankfully. 'How are things anyway?'

'Chaotic as usual.' She paused, shouted a threat at Tommy for something he was doing, then came back on the line. 'Did you find a dentist?'

'Uh – well, I got a name. A man called Raddock. I'll make an appointment tomorrow.'

'Good.' There was a sudden rumpus in the background. 'Damn, the dog's been sick again. I'll need to go.'

Mary hung up as he started to say goodbye. Replacing the receiver with a grimace, Thane turned away from the desk as Moss came back in.

'The car's waiting for you out front,' reported Moss. 'Who were you calling anyway – headquarters?'

'Not the way you mean,' said Thane glumly, and left him.

Jane and Arthur Gibb lived in a small split-level bungalow in Ayer Crescent, where property values were low by Monkswalk standards because it over-looked the local cemetery. The house was white with blue paintwork, the garden was compact and neat, and a matching blue Alfa Romeo coupé was parked in the driveway.

The rain had stopped and the puddles were begin-ning to dry as the Millside car stopped outside. Thane glanced around, told the driver to let him know if anything came over the radio, then headed for the house door.

A three-note set of chimes rang when he pushed the bell. After a moment the door opened and a tall, slim woman with long brunette hair looked out. She wore yellow trousers and a loose, matching top, was about thirty, and had dark, unfriendly eyes.

'Mrs Gibb?'

She nodded, then raised a bored, disinterested eyebrow as she saw the waiting police car. 'Oh, no . . . if it's another motoring charge I'll scream! I told Arthur . . .'

'I'm C.I.D., not traffic department. Is your husband at home?'

'Yes.' She frowned, then opened the door wider. 'You'd better come in, I suppose.' Thane did, then followed her down the hallway. It opened out into an open-plan lounge and dining room. 'Police, Arthur,' she announced as they entered. 'He says it isn't about the car.'

'That's a change,' came a sardonic voice. Arthur Gibb rose from the depths of a plastic-weave armchair, a drink in one hand. A gaunt-faced man with thinning fair hair, he wore petrol-blue slacks with a pastel-pink shirt and matching tie. 'What's the trouble?'

For a moment Thane didn't answer, blinking at the room. One entire wall was a painted mural of a bullfight, the action in the best blood-and-sand tradition. Propped against it to one side was a six-foot-high plush velvet teddy bear. The carpet was a coarse green matting, the furniture around either plastic weave and oddly shaped or utilitarian white-painted wood.

'Jane did the wall – that's her hobby. The bear's name is Fred,' said Gibb conversationally. 'Well, I asked what this was all about.'

'A letter we found.' Thane took the scented blue envelope from his pocket. 'Recognize it?'

'Maybe.' Gibb came over, eyes narrowing as Thane took out the letter and held it towards them.

40

'I wrote that,' admitted Jane Gibb slowly.

'And it was private,' snapped Gibb. 'So how did you get it?'

'Margaret Barclay's body was taken out of the river today. There was unopened mail at her apartment.' Thane waited for their reaction. Gibb made a faint sucking noise between his teeth, but his wife said nothing, only moistening her lips a little.

'So she's dead.' Gibb sipped his glass, grimaced, then gestured towards one of the plastic shapes. 'You'd better sit down. Like a drink?'

Thane shook his head.

'Well, I'm having another,' declared Gibb. 'Jane?'

She nodded. 'Gin and something.'

Emptying his glass at a gulp, Gibb crossed the room, patted the teddy bear absently on the head as he passed, and opened a cupboard.

'What's your name?' he demanded, reaching for a bottle and not looking round.

'Thane.' Lowering himself carefully into the flimsy plastic frame, he watched Jane Gibb curl herself into the chair opposite. For the first time he realized that her feet were bare, the toenails painted bronze. 'The letter interested me.'

'I'll bet,' commented Gibb cynically. He finished pouring the drinks, brought one over to his wife, then remained standing with his own. 'I've heard of you. Since when did chief inspectors get involved with suicides?'

'You think she killed herself?' asked Thane mildly.

'She was the type who might,' shrugged Gibb. 'Anyway, you said . . .' He stopped and glanced at his wife. 'No, he didn't, did he? Chief Inspector, there's an old tag line – did she fall or was she pushed. Which was it?'

'Neither.' Thane eased further back in the plastic

cradle. It was more comfortable than it looked. 'She was strangled first.'

Jane Gibb's hand jerked a little. Some of her drink slopped from the glass on to the yellow trousers. She ignored it, her face unchanged, her voice controlled. 'When did it happen?'

'About a week ago.'

'Before we wrote the letter.' Gibb pursed his lips briefly. 'We tried phoning a few times first, but couldn't get a reply.' He grimaced. 'Well, now we know why.'

Thane nodded. 'When did you see her last?'

'Ten days ago, when she looked in here – briefly.' Jane Gibb frowned while one bare foot absently rubbed the other. 'Better understand this now, Chief Inspector. Margaret Barclay wasn't any kind of close friend, just someone we knew.'

'Someone who called herself a witch,' said Thane quietly.

'And you read our letter.' Gibb gave a faint, understanding nod. 'Look, I run an advertising and public relations firm. That's a hard-headed world to survive in. So – yes, Jane and I have had a dabble at this witchcraft business. But only for kicks. Margaret Barclay –' he shook his head firmly – 'she was for real. There were times when she could scare me.'

'How long had you known her?'

Jane Gibb answered, brushing a strand of hair back from her forehead. 'About a year. She did a couple of jobs for our agency – we didn't use her again, but we kept in touch.'

Her husband nodded. 'After a while she invited us along to a witchcraft coven. It was something different, so we went a couple of times.'

'Where?' asked Thane. In the background the giant teddy bear seemed to be staring straight at him as a trick of the light made its glassy eyes glitter.

'First time, about six months ago, was behind that cemetery across the road – which was a real surprise,' grunted Gibb. 'After that, in a wood a few miles out of town. She called them "open" meetings, which meant the regulars brought guests along. Anonymous guests. She said nobody, even in the coven, would know who we were.' He thought for a moment. 'There were maybe twenty people at each meeting.'

'People you knew?'

'After dark, with half of them prancing around naked and everyone wearing fancy masks?' Gibb snorted and shook his head. 'Not a chance. Nothing much happened anyway. We drank a lot of wine, some of them danced round a character dressed up like a pantomime bull, and a few couples faded away to – well, that was their business.'

'And now you're organizing your own coven?'

Jane Gibb stirred and shifted uneasily in her chair. 'That's what the letter said. But it was just going to be a fun thing for some friends.'

'With Margaret Barclay along as star attraction,' admitted Gibb. He scowled down at the matting, his gaunt face tightening. 'Thane, you don't have to believe this. But once I'd posted that letter it suddenly didn't seem such a good idea. I'm not the super-stitious type, but the way those witchcraft people believe, the serious ones, can get at you. When they start talking about curses and spells they mean it. I was ready to back out. Our "coven" idea is dead as of now.'

Jane Gibb nodded agreement, sipped her glass, then asked, 'Chief Inspector, why was she murdered?'

'We don't know yet.' With sudden relief he heard the car horn blare outside and began to lever himself up out of the plastic. 'There's not much in her apart-ment that helps.'

'What about her workshop?' queried Gibb. He saw

Thane's blank reaction. 'She didn't have a car, but she rented a lock-up garage somewhere near Chelor Grove. That's where she did any work that came her way – though not many people knew it. She kept quiet in case the landlord would want a higher rent.'

'You know where it is?'

Gibb shook his head. 'She told us about it, that's all.'

The car horn sounded again, two short blasts this time and more urgently.

'We'll find it,' said Thane. Then, as Gibb moved to go with him towards the door, he added, 'I'll probably be back.'

'Why?' queried Jane Gibb sharply. 'We checked on this witchcraft thing. It isn't against the law – not on its own, anyway.'

'Murder is,' he reminded quietly.

The teddy bear in the corner seemed to leer its own answer as he went out.

The last of the puddles had gone and a rising wind was whipping the last broken fragments of cloud across the sky. Thane reached the car, climbed aboard, and turned questioningly to the driver as soon as he'd slammed the door.

'Thought I'd better get you out of there, sir,' said the man cheerfully. 'Control called us with a message from Inspector Moss.' He squinted down at the clipboard on his lap. 'Timed 18.52. It says: "Tulley collected and wish you were here." That's all, sir.'

'It's enough.' Thane settled back with a sigh, brought out his cigarettes, and offered them.

'I'm trying to give them up,' said the driver sadly. He glanced curiously towards the house. 'How was it in there, sir? Luxury style?'

'Empty style,' said Thane shortly. 'Let's get back.'

The driver glanced at him, read the signs, and set

the car moving. As they pulled away the radio began murmuring again. Eastern Division was looking for a missing child and wanted one of the dog-handler vans.

Thane mentally wished them luck, lit his cigarette, and concentrated on his own problems.

Dusk was edging in over the grimy lines of tenement buildings as they reached Millside, and lights were already burning throughout the police office building. Going up, he found Phil Moss using a telephone in the main C.I.D. room, an unusual number of men waiting around. Moss waved a hand, finished his conversation quickly, and slammed down the receiver.

'That's it,' he reported briskly. 'I sent Beech over to Central Division to collect Drew Tulley. They've just left for here.'

'Central Division?' Thane glanced around, suddenly realizing what was wrong. Day-shift and night-shift teams were around in almost equal numbers.

'Uh-huh. Central spotted Tulley's car near George Square. He was coming back to it with a girl when they picked him up.'

'Good.' Thane nodded absently, then frowned. 'Why aren't the day shift off duty?'

'Something else happened while you were roaming,' said Moss dryly. 'Headquarters put all divisions on standby. Some wit with an Irish accent phoned a tip that there's going to be a bomb explosion tonight. Except he didn't say where – and he hung up before they could trace the call.'

Thane swore, thinking of the overtime sheet. Beckoning Moss to follow, he went into his room.

'Well, what happened out there?' asked Moss, back-heeling the door shut again.

45

'Nothing I liked.' Thane told him the story in a few short sentences and shrugged. 'On the surface they come down to two people who've run out of thrills.'

'And you believe them?' asked Moss shrewdly.

'I'm not certain, but probably.' Thane stopped and shook his head in open bewilderment. 'Phil, all this witchcraft idiocy was brushed under the carpet centuries ago.'

'But the carpet's been changed,' muttered Moss. He pointed at the desk. 'Want rid of that suitcase?'

'Not yet.' Going over, Thane opened it again and looked at the jumbled contents. Pensively, he unscrewed the lid of the glass jar and sniffed the contents.

'I tried that,' said Moss. 'It stinks, whatever it is.'

Nodding, Thane dipped his fingers into the pale, creamy mixture, felt the smooth textures, then wiped his hand clean again with an instinctive disgust. Closing the jar, he shut the case and dumped it in a corner of the room.

'One thing you'd better do before Tulley gets here is call headquarters,' warned Moss as he finished. 'Buddha Ilford called twice. I made soothing noises, but . . .'

'But now it's my turn.' Thane grimaced at the thought, dropped into his chair, and reached for the telephone. The switchboard connected him quickly and Buddha Ilford's voice was grating in his ear before he had time to light a fresh cigarette.

'Where the devil have you been?' demanded the C.I.D. boss peevishly. 'Out riding on a broomstick somewhere? All I get from anyone about this Barclay murder sounds like a Hallowe'en tale. What's going on?'

'Not as much as I'd like,' admitted Thane. 'But we've got her boyfriend now.'

'Thanks to Central Division, as I heard it,' grunted

46

Ilford. 'Well, try and sit on the witchcraft prattle as far as the press are concerned. They've started nibbling, but this bomb scare may take their tiny minds off it.'

'If anything develops I'll let you know straight away,' promised Thane.

'You'd better,' grunted Ilford. 'Now clear the line. If any bomb does go off I want to know about it.'

'Yes, sir.' Dutifully, Thane hung up. He had his own idea about exactly where he'd have put a bomb at that moment. Down the back of Ilford's chair.

'Chewed you?' Moss belched sympathetically.

'A shade.' Shivering a little, feeling strangely cold, he glanced to check the window was closed. 'Phil, put a couple of the night-shift team on locating this lock-up garage.'

'That should be easy enough.' Moss paused, looking at him oddly. 'Anything wrong with you?'

'I'm fine. Why?'

'No real reason. Forget it.' Moss twisted a grin and went out.

Sitting back, Thane lit the cigarette he'd been wanting. But the first taste of the smoke filled him with a sudden disgust and he stubbed it quickly. Shivering again, he looked at his hands. They'd started to shake.

The telephone rang and for once he lifted it gratefully.

'Yes?'

'Doc Williams here.' The police surgeon's voice came laconically over the wire. 'I thought you'd maybe like a preview of the Barclay post-mortem report.'

'I would.' The shaking had spread to his legs. Where a moment before he'd felt cold there was now a damp sweat breaking on his forehead. 'But keep it brief, Doc.'

'All right.' Doc Williams sounded mildly surprised.

47

'Body was a well-nourished female, et cetera. Approximate time of death, seven days ago – and I'm not going to be able to give you better than that. Cause of death, strangulation by ligature with fracture of the hyoid bone and diffused bruising of the deeper tissues of the neck. Positively dead before she went in the river.'

'Any sexual assault?' Thane croaked the words, his lips dry, trying to keep his mind from wandering, the familiar lines of his office beginning to sway.

'No trace of it. But remember that cut on her forehead?' Doc Williams began to warm in enthusiasm. 'I told you it looked interesting. First, I ran a check on tissue samples for blood infiltration. She was still alive when it happened.' He became suddenly confidential. 'Colin, the next bit sounds crazy. How much truth is there in the story she was some kind of witch?'

'She claimed it.' Thane drew a shuddering breath, keeping the telephone to his ear by an effort. His whole body had begun to shake and he felt heat coming off him like a fever. Heat and yet he was cold.

'Good,' crackled Doc Williams' voice. 'I knew I'd heard about that kind of wounding sometime, and I ended up going through some of my old student-days notebooks. It was in medical history class and was called "the cut above the breath". To kill a witch you had to do that first. It robbed her of her powers.'

Thane sat silent, unable to answer, the room beginning to turn around him in a slow circle, a wave of light-headed nausea sweeping over everything.

'Colin . . .'

He heard it from a long way away while strange shapes began to dance before his eyes. A giant bear leered close, receded, and became a snarling figure which was half bull, half man. Then, as they vanished, Margaret Barclay's wide-eyed face appeared close with a deep slash across her forehead and a gibbering horror on her lips.

'Colin . . .'

It was louder, nearer this time, and a different voice.

The visions shivered, and he caught a swimming picture of Phil Moss coming towards him from the door. D.C. Beech and a stranger were behind him.

Then the world dissolved again, a wind was roaring in his ears, and his mind seemed to explode.

They caught him as he pitched across the desk, the phone still in his hand.

Chapter Three

Most of the time he had a vague idea of what was happening. Faces came and went, people moved him, held him down, forced him up. A bright light shone briefly into his eyes and something sharp stuck into his arm. But the real and the unreal blended, strange shapes swam through rushing, pulsing waves of swirling unreality, misted confusion varied with moments of dazzling clarity.

Very gradually the feeling began to fade. He was lying on his back, feeling strangely comfortable, looking up at his room's grimy ceiling, the single light bulb glaring down from its Corporation-issue glass shade.

'He'll do,' said a voice which shouldn't have been there.

Colin Thane turned his head. Shirt-sleeved and grinning, Doc Williams was standing over him. Beside the police surgeon, Phil Moss looked down with an expression of relief on his thin face.

He was lying on the camp bed usually kept in a cupboard for times when a long job meant snatching an hour's sleep. They'd removed his jacket and tie and his right arm was oddly painful below the shoulder.

'Doc . . .' Thane licked his lips and tried to move.

'Stay there and shut up,' said Doc Williams firmly.

'You've given us enough trouble, and you've still got a pulse like a runaway train. So take it easy.'

'All right. But . . .'

'He wants to know what happened,' grunted Moss, relief giving place to a satisfied lack of sympathy. 'Well, for a start it was your own damned fault.'

'Plus a bit of do-it-yourself black magic,' added the police surgeon, lighting a cigarette. 'Was it rough?'

'I wouldn't recommend it,' said Thane fervently.

'And I wouldn't blame you,' agreed Doc Williams. 'Still, it's fascinating. With any luck I'll get an article out of this for one of the medical journals. You were on a drug trip, almost LSD style.' He smiled a little at the look of disbelief which crossed Thane's face. 'I mean it. And you can thank Phil that we brought you out so quickly.'

Moss shrugged with a vague embarrassment. 'Get on with it. You said he should rest.'

'He can listen,' said the police surgeon, unabashed. 'After the way I got rushed here he owes me that much. Then, when I'm finished, you're going to buy me a drink – a large drink, and I don't mean beer.'

'Doc,' pleaded Thane. 'What was it?'

'Alkaloid poisoning, probably the hyoscyamine group.' Doc Williams began to pull on his jacket. 'When I arrived you showed most of the symptoms from contracted pupils onwards. When it hit you first you felt generally ill and began to lose muscular control. Then you had visual hallucinations leading to a lot worse. Am I right?'

Thane nodded, his mouth tightening at the memory.

'Perfect textbook reactions.' Satisfied, Doc Williams bent down and grasped Thane's right hand. 'How did you gash those fingers?'

'On a pin this afternoon. But . . .'

'Phil says you were playing around with a jar of muck from Margaret Barclay's suitcase.' The police surgeon released Thane's hand, reached over to the desk, and produced the jar. 'This one.'

'I handled it, yes.' Puzzled, Thane stared at them. 'Maybe about – well, fifteen minutes before this started.'

Doc Williams sighed. 'Some people never learn. When you played around you almost certainly absorbed some of the cream directly into the blood-stream through those cuts. I'll have the stuff analysed. But from the way it looks and smells I'll take a bet that cream is loaded with alkaloid-based extracts. How's your arm?'

'Sore.'

'It should be. I had to slap you a full twenty-five milligram jab of neostigmine, and you weren't too cooperative.'

'I'll believe you.' Thane propped himself up on one elbow and gave a perplexed glance towards Moss. 'But if the stuff could do this to me . . .'

'I'm thinking the same,' agreed Moss, frowning at the jar. 'What did she do with it?'

'I wouldn't know,' confessed Doc Williams. 'But I wouldn't prescribe it as any kind of rub for a sore back.' He dropped the jar into his medical bag, snapped the bag shut, and considered Thane again. 'When you're ready, send me over the rest of the stuff in that suitcase. It might be interesting. Right now – any sense in telling you to go home?'

'With all this going on?' Stubbornly, Thane shook his head.

'Wasted effort, as I thought.' Doc Williams shrugged a resigned acceptance. 'We'll compromise. You rest here for a spell – then go easy.'

'I will.' Thane glanced towards Moss. 'Where's Tulley?'

'Parked in a cell,' said Moss, untroubled. 'He'll keep.'

52

'Some of my customers need the same treatment,' murmured Doc Williams. He hefted his bag, ready to leave. 'Colin, how much of my post-mortem rundown registered with you?'

'All of it. Including the part about her being "cut above the breath",' confirmed Thane soberly. 'You're sure you've got it right?'

'I could show you the lecture notes,' nodded the police surgeon amiably. 'In those days I was the original keen young student and our forensic lecturer was wandering in his dotage. He had a thing about black magic. One of his pet theories was that all lighthouses should be blown up because they were camouflaged phallic symbols. But he quoted cases – a slash above the breath meant across the forehead. Afterwards, when the witch was helpless, she could be judicially strangled and burned.' He stopped, realized what he'd said, and shrugged. 'I said burned. Not dumped in the nearest river.'

But otherwise it was the same execution pattern. Thane swore under his breath.

'Anything else, Doc?'

'No – her regular health was pretty good.'

Moss stirred. 'How about her teeth?'

'You too?' The police surgeon raised his eyes towards the ceiling in despair. 'I checked. They were fine apart from a couple of temporary stoppings in cavities.'

'She'd been having treatment.' Thane lay back on the camp bed, eyes half-closed. 'Thanks, Doc – for everything.'

'Any time.' The police surgeon winked at him, took Moss firmly by the elbow, and turned him towards the door. 'Time for that drink you promised. We'll call it in lieu of fee.'

They left with Moss still grumbling. As the door clicked shut Thane gave a long, thankful sigh and didn't move for a spell. Eventually he got up, splashed water over his face in the tiny washroom which lay off his office, folded the camp bed back into its cupboard, then sat behind his desk.

Telephones rang outside. He heard footsteps regularly approach his door, stop outside, and quietly go away again. But no one entered and he was glad. Margaret Barclay's suitcase had given him a glimpse of hell in a way he needed time to forget.

At last he glanced at his watch. Startled, he realized almost two hours had passed since he'd called Buddha Ilford – two wasted hours. Grimacing, he flicked the intercom switch.

'Sir?' The orderly at the other end answered quicker than Thane could ever remember. He smiled a little, wondering just what sort of sentry duty Moss had arranged on him.

'The moment D.I. Moss gets back tell him to bring Tulley in here,' he ordered. 'The rest of you stop pussyfooting around and get back to work.'

He closed the switch. Outside, in the main office, he heard someone give a sardonic cheer. The sound made him chuckle. Things were back to normal.

Phil Moss arrived after a few minutes. He gave Thane a single, narrow-eyed glance, nodded his approval, then beckoned over his shoulder. Following him in, escorted by a bland-faced Detective Constable Beech and looking tense and unhappy, Drew Tulley was stocky and sallow. Long black hair brushed his collar as he glanced around, one hand nervously fingering the canary-yellow tie he wore with a dark grey suit which had narrow lapels and a four-button front.

'I've been talking with him,' said Moss without preliminaries. 'Just thought it would save time.' He finished with a fractional, negative headshake.

'A chair for Mr Tulley,' said Thane neutrally. Obediently, Beech swung a chair behind the man. Its edge tapped him behind the knees and Tulley sat down quickly.

'I didn't do it,' he began without prompting in a quick, anxious voice. 'I didn't kill her – don't know a thing about it.' He darted a nervous, bird-like glance at Moss. 'I didn't even know she was dead till he told me.'

'That's what he says,' confirmed Moss with no particular enthusiasm. 'He took Margaret Barclay home around ten o'clock last Monday night. She left his car outside Chelor Grove and he drove straight home.'

'It's the truth.' Tulley's manner took on a shade of truculence. 'And if you're planning on keeping me here I want a lawyer. I'm not going back to that cell.'

Behind him, Beech grinned. Thane stayed straight-faced and nodded sympathetically. 'We don't rise to five-star accommodation, Mr Tulley. And it's my fault you were kept waiting. But nobody said you were being charged with anything, did they?'

'No.' Tulley swallowed and became more hopeful. 'If you put it like that I – well, I don't mind, I suppose. And I saw how you were when they brought me up before.'

'Forget that.' Thane's manner hardened a little at the reminder. 'What matters is you were brought here to assist with inquiries. Agreed?'

Tulley nodded and tried to force a smile. 'If I can, yes. But . . .'

'We'll find out.' Thane nursed a pencil between his fingers for a moment, then pointed it. 'Were you in her apartment that night?'

'We had a drink there before we went to the Foulis party.' Tulley's self-assurance grew. 'I'll bet the old bag on the ground floor told you that already – she'd be at her periscope.'

'If you mean Mrs Polson, she was out,' said Thane curtly. He tossed the pencil aside. It rolled and clattered to the floor. 'Then, after the party, you say you brought Margaret Barclay back, dropped her off, and drove straight to your own place. But Mrs Polson still wasn't home to see that – and you live alone.'

Tulley went a shade paler. 'Somebody might have noticed me.'

'Beech?'

D.C. Beech shook his head. 'We've tried, sir. No luck, yet, either way.'

'So we've a problem,' murmured Thane. 'How long had you been going around with Margaret Barclay?'

Tulley licked his lips. 'Three months, not much more.'

'Sleeping with her?'

'Now and then.' The man grinned uneasily. 'We were both over twenty-one, Chief Inspector. Anyway, it was finished – tailing off.'

'Meaning you'd quarrelled?'

The yellow tie was tugged again so that the knot slipped down. 'Not the way you think. I – well, I'd decided to slide out, though I didn't tell her. That's the truth.'

'Convince me,' invited Thane bluntly.

Outside, a patrol car started up. The crew were in a hurry and the car's siren began wailing as it pulled away. Mouth twitching, Tulley listened as if hypnotized till the sound faded.

'We're waiting,' said Moss sharply.

'Sorry.' Tulley shivered a little, then seemed to make up his mind. 'You know she fooled around with this witchcraft stuff. Well, she wanted to get me involved and wouldn't take no for an answer.' He sniffed indignantly. 'In my line of business? If I had, if people ever discovered, I'd be out of a job overnight.'

56

'Mr Tulley sells Christmas cards,' explained Moss in a dead-pan fashion.

'It's the order season for them and we wholesale to the trade,' agreed Tulley earnestly. 'But the firm handles greeting cards for all occasions – Easter cards, the lot. I've the best order book in the sales team and top commission. The boss has dropped a hint about needing a new sales director.' He spread his hands wide. 'Do I look like I'd cut my own throat?'

'I wouldn't say you're the type,' murmured Thane. He got up, went over to the window, and looked out at the night. A solitary drunk was weaving along under the streetlamps, instinct taking him home. 'Did she ever name the other people in her coven?'

'No, though I asked her,' confessed Tulley. 'But she wouldn't talk about them – she said I'd find out soon enough if I joined.'

'What about other men – anyone who might have a grudge?'

Wearily, Tulley shook his head. 'She'd been around, that's all I knew. But I've been thinking about that Monday night. She told me before we went to the Foulis place that she'd have to leave early.'

'Why?'

'Her story was she had a headache.' Tulley grimaced. 'When we got there I wanted to stay. There were a couple of good prospects at that party – possible contacts for orders.'

'But you took her home like a gentleman,' said Thane dryly. 'Quite a strain. Why do you think she wanted back?'

'Now?' Tulley shrugged. 'Maybe she'd someone else coming over. Maybe – well, I was tired of her. It could have been mutual.'

Thane nodded. 'All right, that's it for now.'

'And I can go?' Tulley shoved his chair back quickly.

'Later. For the moment, we'll want your finger-prints. And a full statement. But maybe by morning . . .'

'Morning?' Eyes widening, Tulley clenched his fists. 'You can't . . .'

'We can,' corrected Moss acidly. 'Laddy, look on it as a free night's bed and breakfast and no service charge.'

'But my job!' Tulley showed signs of panic. 'My boss . . .'

'Tell him you were doing your duty as a citizen,' said Thane helpfully. 'Phil, take him and get those fingerprints sent to headquarters. Beech, you stay.'

Close to tears, Tulley was led out. Closing the door again, D.C. Beech waited with an expression of inno-cence on his young face. But his mind was churning over various possibilities, including some of the items in his last expense sheet.

'You picked him up,' said Thane shortly. 'What do you think?'

Thankfully, Beech relaxed. 'He wouldn't have the guts, sir. Not to strangle her.'

Thane nodded, the words echoing his own feeling.

'Frank Foulis came here,' he said after a moment. 'You ruffled his feathers dragging him out of that washroom.'

Beech considered that solemnly. 'You told me to see him and not to waste time, sir. I – ah – maybe forced the pace a bit, but I thought that was what you wanted.'

'Any time you think it causes trouble,' said Thane caustically, trying to keep back a twinkle. 'Next time, remember that Monkswalk neds are high-class neds. You act polite, you behave like they're your God-appointed betters. If you arrest them you make sure the handcuffs are clean first. Understood?'

'Yes, sir.' Beech nodded happily.

'Good.' Thane leaned against the crime map. 'Then you can go and finish checking Tulley's story, just in case.'

'Now, sir?' Beech looked hurt. 'I'm due off duty when this bomb scare ends.'

'You volunteered.' Thane eyed him frostily. 'Move.'

Beech moved, almost colliding with Moss as the latter came back in. Thane crossed to his desk and flicked the intercom switch.

'I want the duty car brought round,' he ordered. 'Inspector Moss is going with me.'

'Where?' demanded Moss suspiciously as the switch closed.

'Monkswalk,' Thane told him. 'We've to see the beat cop. And there's that lock-up garage, when it's been found.'

Moss frowned. 'I can cope on my own. You were to take things easy.'

'But I need some fresh air.' Thane lifted his overcoat from its peg, saw the expression on Moss's face, and grinned. 'Phil, you look like a mother hen that just laid a square egg. Hurt and confused. Stop fussing and come on.'

Moss sniffed, belched disapprovingly, and followed him out.

Constable Daniel Seaforth had twenty-seven years' police service and was a bulky, grey-haired man as Highland as heather. The moonlight glinted on his tunic buttons and showed a row of war-service ribbons above one breast pocket. Past the age where promotion was a prospect, he didn't bother to hide his disgust about Monkswalk.

'Och, I'd rather be in town among the neds any day,' he rumbled wistfully. 'You know them an' they know you. Out here, Chief Inspector? The men rush aroun' making money and the women rush aroun' spending it. A few are all right – usually the ones who've really got money. But the rest usually make me want to throw up.'

Colin Thane nodded with a touch of sympathy. A long-service beat cop like Seaforth probably had a take home pay of twenty pounds a week. The basic antagonism was natural.

The wind blew a rustle of dry autumn leaves round their feet, sending them scurrying along the roadway. The C.I.D. car had rendezvoused with Seaforth's Panda patrol car, a blue and white striped Ford, in Veldon Drive. It was a quiet stretch of road about half a mile from Chelor Grove, the houses hidden behind thick hedges. That wind had a dull edge, though Seaforth didn't feel it. He was standing in front of the Panda car, warming his backside in the heat rising from the radiator grille.

'Much work in it?' asked Moss, edging round to use Thane as a windbreak.

'Plenty o' petty stuff,' admitted Seaforth. 'Motoring offences, drunks, old wives complainin' that the next-door dog lifts its leg on their front step. But the bigger things usually get hushed up.'

'Preserving the image,' murmured Thane. 'How much do you pick up on the gossip grapevine?'

'Damned little, sir.' Seaforth shook his head sadly. 'It was bad enough when we walked the beat. Now, wi' the cars, it's ruddy impossible.'

The two Millside men exchanged a glance. It was the old story. The Panda radio-car system of one-man patrols covered more ground and meant a quick response to trouble. But the basic contact had lessened – though the other side of the coin was the need for maximum stretch from a force now five hundred under authorized strength and losing more every time outside industry won another wage increase.

'But you'll still hear a few things?' suggested Moss hopefully.

'Aye.' Seaforth twisted a grin. 'I know where there's a wife-swapping party most Saturdays. Or who's most likely to be brought home drunk in a taxi. That sort o' thing. Plus an idea o' which families are up to their ears in debt. There's plenty o' the "fur coats and nae drawers" stuff around here.'

'And witchcraft?' Thane asked sharply.

Seaforth frowned, hesitated, and rubbed his backside against the grille as if to speed the thought process. 'I'd a notion it was happenin', yes.'

From a few yards down the street the duty car's driver flashed his lights twice, which meant Control was calling. Grunting, Moss padded towards it.

'Go on,' encouraged Thane.

'Well, a while back there were some tombstones pushed over at the cemetery. Kids, I thought – till I foun' a cockerel lyin' near them wi' its head chopped off. Then there was the night I came back to the car an' found a clay doll propped against the windscreen wi' a pin stuck through its belly.'

Thane whistled softly. As if in response, something large swept low overhead in a fast, heavy wing-beat. It had to be an owl, but he shivered.

'You know what happened?' Seaforth gave a rumbling chuckle. 'I stayed fine but the sergeant went sick. Mind you, he'd been at his cousin's wedding the night before, an' his cousin is charge-hand at a distillery. But –' he paused, considered Thane thoughtfully for a moment – 'well, I'll show you something, if it stays between you an' me.'

'It will.' Curious, Thane joined him as he stooped and flashed a hand-torch low on the car's radiator grille. A small sprig of leafy twig was tied there by wire.

'Rowan tree,' said Seaforth with a shamefaced grin.

61

'When I was a laddie up in Argyll my mother always kept a branch o' rowan above the cottage door. Most Highland folk will tell you there's no better way o' keeping out Auld Hornie.' He flicked out the torch and rose. 'Mind you, I'm not what you'd call superstitious, sir.'

'You believe in insurance,' agreed Thane with a small grin of understanding. 'Now, what about the night the Barclay woman was murdered?'

Seaforth's face folded into gloomier lines. 'The only thing that happened was right here, in Veldon Drive, an' that's why I said meet here. Control called me about 1 a.m. sayin' there was a report of a woman screaming.' He shrugged. 'I couldn't find anything when I arrived – an' the original report was the usual anonymous telephone call.'

'You logged it?'

'Aye.' Sighing, Seaforth eased his cap back on his head. 'Look, sir, that happens, aroun' here. Two nights ago there was a woman wi' no clothes on runnin' like hell and her husband chasin' after her in a car. So I stopped his car. An' what happens? The ruddy woman trots up, says I can get stuffed, an drives off wi' him.' His head shook in bewildered fashion. 'Night beat out here is like bein' keeper at a zoo.'

Moss was coming back from the C.I.D. car. Seeing him, Seaforth glanced significantly at his watch. 'If you're finished, sir, I've a load o' motoring offence summonses to deliver . . .'

Thane nodded. Giving a friendly salute, Seaforth squeezed back into the Panda car's driving seat and set the vehicle moving.

'Could he help?' asked Moss as the roof-mounted police sign disappeared round a bend.

'A little – maybe more than that.' Another car came towards them, travelling fast. A Rolls-Royce, its headlamps swept them briefly, then gravel spattered from the tyres as it swung into a private driveway. 'What did Control want?'

'They'd a message for you from our desk. We've traced Margaret Barclay's studio – that garage the Gibbs talked about. I've got the address.' Moss pulled his jacket tighter against the wind. 'And the bomb scare is over. Southern Division picked up a character who had an airline bag full of gelignite. He wanted to blow up the local bookmaker.'

'Another satisfied customer.' Thane grinned and thumbed towards the car.

The lock-up garage was one of a flat-roofed row located down a pot-holed, unlit lane about a quarter-mile from Chelor Grove. A two-car unit, only the number above the doors distinguished it from its neighbours – plus the fact that a couple of police cars were already drawn up outside.

Thane's car joined them. He got out, told the Mill-side driver to pass their arrival to Control, then headed over with Moss at his side. A plain-clothes night-team man was on guard at a small service door to one side. He opened it. Thane stepped through into the brightly lit interior, then stopped, surprised.

'Were you two born in a field?' complained a famil-iar voice as he looked around. The whole broad two-car space had been converted into a studio area, spartan in style but furnished down to a strip of carpet on the concrete floor. 'Colin, get that streak of misery behind you to shut the flaming door. I'm half-frozen as it is.'

'You got here fast, Dan,' said Thane, with the begin-nings of a frown.

Behind him Moss closed the door with a snort. But kept his attention on the figure who'd risen from being on his knees beside an overturned drawing board and easel. Bulky, a cigarette dangling from his mouth and ash trickling down his ancient sheepskin jacket, Superintendent Dan Laurence was head of the city's Scientific Bureau. He had a mop of white hair with a yellow streak of nicotine staining at the front. 'Mind telling me how?'

'No need to get temperamental,' assured Laurence, coming over with a grin. Behind him, another of the Millside night team was standing near a desk talking to a flush-faced stranger, a tubby little man wearing a homburg hat and a dark overcoat. 'Nobody's been holding out on you.'

'You just happened to be passing?' suggested Moss cynically.

'Uh-huh.' Laurence cradled both hands round his ample paunch, amused at their reaction. 'If you must know, Buddha Ilford sent me to have a look at the Barclay woman's apartment – call it brainpower to the aid o' the Divisional muscle. I was almost there when I heard about this place. I only got here a couple of minutes ago.' The cigarette twitched a fraction as his mouth hardened. 'And it looks like I picked the better bet.'

Looking past him, Thane nodded a sober agreement. The desk drawers lay open with papers strewn around and the broken remains of what looked like an earthenware vase had scattered over the carpet.

'I've radioed for the rest o' my team,' said Laurence. He thumbed towards the stranger. 'That's the landlord – he came along with the key.'

'Phil.' Thane's nod sent his second-in-command drifting in that direction. Then he considered Laurence again. The Scientific boss didn't usually turn up unannounced an a job unless the pressure was on from somewhere. 'Who's pushing this one, Dan?'

Before he answered, Laurence lit a fresh cigarette from the stub of the old one. 'Chief Constable level,

Colin. And same people higher up are worried about what's starting to crawl out of the woodwork.'

'Monkswalk believes in a sanitized image,' said Thane bleakly. 'All right, Dan, what have we got?'

'So far?' Laurence led him over to a small wash-basin and mirror in the far corner. The white porcelain was specked and streaked with red. A heavily blood-stained towel lay on the floor beside it. 'Somebody tried to clean up afterwards. At least, that's how it looks.'

Thane's attention had strayed. 'Not afterwards, Dan.'

He picked up a crumpled wrapper from the floor, smoothed it out, peered round again, then lifted a pair of nylon tights which had been lying in the shadow of a small cupboard. Taking wrapper and tights, Laurence examined them under the lights.

'New, straight out o' the pack, and never been worn. Well?'

'The Panda beat car checked out a report of a woman screaming in Veldon Drive that night.' Thane leaned against the cupboard, his face expressionless under the light, his mind grappling with the tangle of possibilities. 'If it was Margaret Barclay, that could be when she was slashed across the forehead. Suppose she escaped after a scramble. This place is halfway between Veldon Drive and her apartment block.'

Laurence considered far a moment, the cigarette dangling. 'Aye, it could be. She gets here in a mess but not badly hurt. And she's safe, here, or so she thinks. There's an opened half-bottle o' whisky on that desk – one glass. So she could have tried to clean up, had a drink, then . . .' He glanced at the tights in his hand.

'She's a woman,' said Thane patiently. 'Whatever she's going to do next, the tights she's wearing are ripped to hell. And she had a spare pair here. So she starts to change them.'

Laurence pondered and scowled. 'Then your killer comes in before she finishes changing, grabs the pair she just took off and strangles her? Fine – except why did she let him in?'

'I wouldn't know.' Thane ran his finger along the nearest surface and held up the result.

Laurence nodded. 'Dust, plenty of it,' he agreed. 'We may get prints, if he was careless. But I'll check out that blood against her grouping. You could be wrong, Colin. She could have marked him.'

He shrugged, left Laurence to prowl again, and crossed over to the other group. 'Phil?'

'Mr Maurice Fulton – he owns the lock-ups.' Moss used a thin elbow to ease the flustered figure forward.

'That's right.' Fulton ran a finger round his shirt collar. 'And I didn't know a damned thing about this layout, believe me. If I had . . .'

'You don't inspect your property?' asked Thane coldly.

'Not unless someone wants maintenance work.' Fulton bristled a little. 'This is Monkswalk. People prefer privacy.'

'And pay for it?' Thane didn't wait for an answer. 'This is a double garage. Didn't it seem unusual that a woman on her own wanted it?'

'Tell him, Mr Fulton,' said Moss with a tantalizing half-smile.

Fulton sighed. 'She came to me about six months ago with an introduction from – from someone.'

'Who also paid the first year's rent in advance,' murmured Moss. 'Frank Foulis, insurance king. Right, Mr Fulton?'

'Yes.'

Another car had drawn up outside. The service door opened and Dan Laurence's team entered, to be greeted by a staccato bark of orders from the Scientific boss. Half-listening to them, still watching Fulton, Thane stood silent for a moment.

'You know Frank Foulis?' he asked at last.

'From business.' Fulton shifted his feet, embarrassed. 'I did him a favour, that's all. His – well, why he wanted it wasn't my concern, was it?'

Thane shrugged, then glanced at the night-team man. 'Take Mr Fulton home and get a list of the people who rent the other lock-ups.' He turned to Fulton again. 'Keep quiet about this for now. You understand?'

Fulton nodded fervently, jumped a little as the night-team man touched his arm, and quickly followed him out.

'Surprised?' asked Moss mildly. He fumbled in a baggy packet, and carefully rubbed the grime from a loose stomach pill before he popped it in his mouth and swallowed. 'Do we collect Foulis?'

'He'll keep. He's clever enough to know we'd find this place eventually – and we told him we'd want a full statement tomorrow. Let's see what he says in it.'

'Tomorrow is also when you've got him identifying Margaret Barclay's body,' mused Moss. 'Afterwards would be a nice time for the statement.'

'It would.' Thane's eyes strayed again to the Bureau men, now working systematically throughout the studio. 'Then maybe we'll visit his wife. Mrs Foulis doesn't look the type who'd like a witch casting any kind of spell around her husband.'

Dan Laurence came over. Combing a hand through his white hair, he stopped in front of Thane.

'We won't have anything from here for a while, Colin. But one o' my lads brought out a message. Fingerprints you sent in from Drew Tulley match up wi' prints from a glass in the Barclay woman's apartment. All other identifiable prints from there were her own. Does that help?'

'We expected it, but thanks.'

'Colin –' Laurence stayed where he was, oddly embarrassed for a man who had a reputation for having an armour-plated ego – 'about this witchcraft thing. How much do you know about what goes on?'

'Just the stories I got scared with as a kid.'

The kind most youngsters loved to hear and collect. Then forgot as they grew up, or thought they'd forgotten until a movement on a dark night or some quiver of light and shade sparked an uneasy memory.

'I could maybe help.' Laurence looked positively sheepish. 'You see, I know a witch. She's a –' he swallowed – 'well, a sort of distant relative. By marriage, not my side of the family. Lives in a cottage out near Loch Lomond.'

'With a cat?' asked Moss mildly.

Laurence gave him a glare which would have shrivelled most mortals. 'If you must know, she breeds bloody dogs. Colin, I could fix it for you to go and see her. She has a telephone.' He grimaced, still embarrassed. 'We think she's round the twist, but . . .'

'It might help, Dan.' Thane tried to sound more enthusiastic than he felt.

'Right.' Laurence glared at Moss again then made an indignant withdrawal.

'You aren't serious?' Moss was incredulous. 'She'll be some old crone with whiskers and flat feet. Any way . . .'

'Leave it,' said Thane wearily, his tooth suddenly throbbing again. 'Maybe he'll forget. Let's get finished here. I'll take this half, you take the other. Letters, witchcraft stuff, names – you know what we're looking for, Phil. If anything's been left, that is.'

He doubted it. The opened desk and scattered papers told a fairly convincing story.

For almost an hour they worked side by side with the Bureau men. Shelves held thick bundles of design sketches for shops and showrooms, most of them old and dusty. An envelope of film transparencies excited momentary interest but came down to three of Margaret Barclay in a wisp of a bikini and a series of seascape views.

'Nothing,' reported Moss gloomily at the finish. 'Nothing that matters, anyway. There were some kinky charcoal drawings in the cupboard, the Devil and assorted hobgoblins horsing around. Do we want them?'

Thane looked at a few. They were all variations on the same theme, a circle of strange, nightmare creatures dancing round a horned satyr-like figure who lounged on a serpent throne. Crude, perverted in their detail, the sketches might have been peopled straight from his own all too recent nightmares.

'Leave them.' He tossed the sketches aside and felt a sudden need to be in the open air. Turning on his heel, he left the lock-up and went out into the lane and stood far a moment, breathing deeply. Under the pale, cold moonlight the car headlamps shone yellow and the wind through the trees seemed a mocking whisper. Yawning, feeling very tired, he looked along the lane and found it easy to imagine how it must have been when Margaret Barclay came running through the same darkness. Fleeing to imagined safety.

Except something had gone wrong afterwards. Had there already been someone waiting when she entered the studio, someone she'd trusted? Or had that someone come along later? Had Margaret Barclay opened the door expecting to greet a friend who'd arrived to help her?

He swore quietly at the possible inference. Just how many people were involved in it all? Thirteen was the accepted strength of a witchcraft coven. They were one short now in Monkswalk – and whatever they knew, whatever part they'd played, one thing was certain. The twelve left must be frightened people who would stay silent as long as possible.

Maybe to the end.

The garage service door clicked behind him and Moss came out. For a moment the small, lean figure stood equally silent, then his stomach rumbled loudly and for once he muttered an apology.

'Dan's men are packing up,' said Moss after another silence. 'Maybe you should too. You told Doc Williams you'd take it easy, remember?'

Glancing at his watch, Thane nodded wryly. It was already approaching 2 a.m. He fought back another yawn.

'All right. But tomorrow we'll have every man we've got knocking doors around here. And if anyone in Monkswalk tries to pull up the drawbridge on this one . . .' He didn't finish, his mouth a hard line.

'What about Tulley?'

'Unless something special turns up, we'll let him go in the morning. Make it in time for him to get to work – but we'll keep tabs on him.' He didn't try to hide his yawn this time. 'Then I want the Gibbs brought over to the Barclay apartment. We'll let them look around and see if they feel anything's missing.'

They reached the C.I.D. car still last in the row. Standing beside it, the uniformed driver had his door open and was staring in with a strange expression on his face.

'Something wrong?'

The man, a tall Viking-built blond named Ericson, turned with a start and licked his lips.

70

'I – I went round the back o' the garages a moment, sir. It's been a long night and . . .'

'Well?' Thane came nearer, puzzled. Ericson was an easy-going character who only cared about gear ratios and carburettors.

'I was only away for a moment so I didn't lock the car and . . .'

Thane shoved him aside, swore softly, and picked up the shape lying in the passenger seat under the glow of the panel lights.

It was a small, crudely shaped doll made out of modelling clay. A long brass pin had been stuck through the head from right to left.

Ericson was cursing now, shining a torch around.

'Forget it,' said Thane bitterly.

He tossed the doll into the car's parcel shelf, nursed his tooth with his tongue, and climbed aboard.

Mary was asleep when he got home. So were the kids, and the dog hardly bothered to raise its head from its basket when he looked in the kitchen for a couple of aspirin.

Quietly, smiling a little, he went upstairs, undressed in the dark, and slipped into his side of the bed. For a moment he lay there, the warmth of Mary's body reaching his own, listening to her soft, regular breath.

He wanted to think.

But he was asleep before he could start.

Chapter Four

Slobbering, large and hot-breathed, the shape hit him heavily and began clawing at his pyjama-clad shoulder. Which was routine. Grunting, quarter-awake, Colin Thane shoved the sixty-pound weight of boxer dog away as it tried to lick his stubbled face.

'Get lost, Clyde,' he yawned, realizing Mary's side of the bed was empty and the sun already coming in bright through a gap in the curtains. There were noises from the kitchen, and he winced as he saw the bedside clock. It was eight-thirty, the time when he'd planned to be at Millside to pick up the day's threads.

The dog made a dive for his bare feet as he got out of bed. He swore at it half-heartedly, fumbled for a cigarette, then heard the front door bang as if it was coming off its hinges. The kids were on their way to school.

A minute later there were footsteps on the stair and Mary came in. She was dark-haired, small, and had a smooth fresh complexion. Even in the old red dressing gown which was her pre-breakfast uniform she still showed the kind of figure no woman with two school-age children had any right to retain.

'He rose, rested and refreshed.' She inspected him, grimaced, then let it slip to a smile. 'Why doesn't it happen to you?' Clyde tried to wrestle with her and she shoved him down. 'Phil's here.'

'And we're feeding him?' He could guess what that meant as he kissed her. Mary's mothering instincts seemed roused immediately Moss appeared on the doorstep. 'Scrambled eggs again?'

'He needs a bland diet.' She put a hand on his chest, fending him off, then considered him carefully. 'Did anything happen to you last night?'

'Nothing special,' he answered warily. 'Why?'

'Phil asked how you were. That usually means something.' She frowned at him a moment longer before she gave up. 'Well, for the record your children said to say hello and they'll maybe see you some time. I'll need to go – Phil's waiting on his breakfast.'

Thane opened his mouth to protest. But she'd already gone. Sighing, he side-stepped a new rush by Clyde and went to wash.

Ten minutes later, when he came downstairs, it was to find Moss nursing a cup of tea between his hands at the kitchen table, his emptied plate pushed to one side.

'Can't your landlady feed you on what you pay her?' demanded Thane, dropping into the chair opposite.

'Not when I'm out early enough to have half a day's work done before you decide to surface,' retorted Moss without a blush. 'Maybe you should have stayed in bed. Look at these.' He lifted a bundle of newspapers from the floor and fanned them across the table.

Black headlines in a variety of typefaces, six depending on circulation figures, met Thane's eyes. From 'Monkswalk Witch Murder' to 'Witch Strangler Dumped Body' all gave the story full page-one treatment. The Southern Division bomber didn't feature in as much as an end-column paragraph.

Thane ruminated over them, clearing enough space for Mary to dump a plate with his dried-up share of the scrambled eggs. He read and ate in silence, gulped some tea as he finished, then shrugged.

'The stories are pretty thin. Nothing in them that's going to cause us problems.'

'But Monkswalk won't like it,' murmured Moss. He winked at Mary as she lit a cigarette. 'We're moving in cultured circles.'

'That makes a change.' She glanced at one of the newspapers then said unexpectedly, 'Well, it's fashionable. Witchcraft, I mean. There was a little man working this street last week selling fertility charms.' She grinned. 'I slammed the door on him.'

A choking noise came from Moss, and he hastily moved things on. 'Anyway, the woman's husband is out of it. Scotland Yard traced him in London through that alimony payment. He works in a Government office and has a cast-iron alibi. The only thing that's worrying him is who'll pay for the funeral.'

Thane grimaced, then munched a slice of toast. 'Any notion why they broke up?'

'General incompatibility – she threw things.' Moss showed a bachelor's disgust at the idea. 'Another loose end tied up is that Scientific Branch say the bloodstains at the garage were the same group as Margaret Barclay's. But they drew a blank on fingerprints.'

Thane shrugged. He'd expected it would be that way. 'Tulley?'

'Still nothing to back his story. But I turned him loose like you said, with a man tailing him.'

'Right,' murmured Thane. 'Then we start off again at why Margaret Barclay had to leave the Foulis party early. Take it she got rid of Tulley. Then – well, she went somewhere.'

'Like a coven meeting?' asked Mary from the background. 'They're supposed to be late-night, aren't they?'

He stared at her, then nodded. It had been under his nose, waiting to be realized. A Monkswalk coven meeting would take priority over anything else in Margaret Barclay's life.

'Then what happened afterwards . . .?' Moss didn't finish.

'Could have been a ritual killing,' agreed Thane in a chilled, deliberate tone. 'If there was trouble within the coven and she was on the receiving end . . . Yes, it fits. How many outsiders would know about that "cut above the breath" business?'

Frowning, Moss considered for a moment, decided to stay uncommitted, and instead glanced pointedly at the kitchen clock.

'You wanted Arthur Gibb and his wife at Chelor Grove. They'll be there at nine-thirty.'

It was already 9 a.m. Swallowing a last mouthful of tea, Thane started to rise. Mary stopped him, vaguely embarrassed.

'How long will it take you?'

'With the Gibbs?' He shrugged. 'Fifteen, maybe twenty minutes should be enough. Why?'

She relaxed. 'Just that you've a dental appointment for ten-fifteen. I made it.'

'In the middle of all this?' He stifled a groan. 'Who's it with anyway?'

'The dentist you told me about, Mr Raddock. Ten-fifteen was the only time he could see you.' She eyed him defensively. 'I knew you'd forget to do anything about it.'

Moss grunted a cynical agreement. But a sudden, longshot idea stirred in Thane's mind.

'You made the appointment last night?'

She nodded. 'I phoned about seven. He'd an evening surgery.'

'And you gave my name.'

'To his receptionist, yes.' She was puzzled. But he

saw a new look of interest in Moss's face and knew he understood.

'Mary, did you tell her my job?'

'No. Just that you'd toothache.'

He thought of the doll placed in the duty car, of the pin driven through its cheeks, but said nothing. 'Phil, what's your transport situation?' he asked instead.

Moss shrugged. 'A traffic car gave me a lift here.'

'We'll take my car.' An elderly, rusting Austin, he and Mary used it on alternate days. 'I'll drop you at the station. Check through the overnight book, stall any cases that don't look important, make sure we'll have enough men on the door-to-door checks, and then get those statements from Frank Foulis and his wife.'

'That's all?' queried Moss bleakly.

'For now,' grinned Thane. 'But I'll keep in touch.'

Mary came with them to the front door and kissed him as they left.

Then she went back to the kitchen and began clearing up, her eyes troubled. She'd been married long enough to accept the normal run of risks. But this time, for a reason she couldn't understand, she felt a thin thread of fear uncurling inside her.

There was a bright blue sky and sunlight had banished the last trace of overnight chill. The breeze had died down till it was only a reminder. But the roads were busy and it was a couple of minutes after nine-thirty when Thane drew up outside Chelor Grove.

Arthur Gibb's blue Alfa Romeo was already parked at the kerb. Cursing, Thane hurried past the uniformed man on duty at the entrance to the apartment block and took the elevator up. Another uniformed man opened the door of Margaret Barclay's apartment and he found Jane and Arthur Gibb sitting patiently on a couch in the lounge.

'Thanks for coming,' said Thane. Gibb was in a tight grey suit with a dark blue shirt and tie. His wife wore a white, lightweight jacket over a high-necked purple dress and had a brief-case on her lap. 'I won't keep you long.'

'Good.' Gibb rose lazily. 'Inspector Moss said you wanted us to take a look around. For what?'

'Anything that might be missing.'

'From here?' Jane Gibb gave what passed for a smile. 'Margaret didn't own anything I'd call worth stealing.'

'Just look around, anyway.'

She shrugged, got up to join her husband, and they followed Thane in a slow procession from room to room, making no secret of their lack of enthusiasm. But when they reached the bedroom Jane Gibb stopped and frowned.

'Any time I was here there was an address book on the dressing table. It had a red leather cover with her initials in gold.'

'You're sure?'

She nodded.

'Mr Gibb?'

Gibb twisted a grimace. 'I wouldn't know. I stay clear of women's bedrooms. Still, if the address book isn't here maybe she took it to her workshop.'

'The studio?' Thane shook his head. 'We've checked there. Anything else missing, Mrs Gibb?'

She looked around slowly. 'No, I don't think so. Except that there should be an old suitcase under the bed.'

'We found it.' Thane watched Gibb wander over to the window. 'Do either of you know Frank Foulis?'

A noise like a chuckle came from Gibb and he glanced round. 'Digging for dirt, Chief Inspector?'

77

'Sorting through it,' he said shortly.

'We heard about him,' agreed Jane Gibb calmly. She stuck her hands deep in her jacket pockets. 'But that was Margaret's business.'

Gibb sighed and looked deliberately at his watch. 'Let's save time, Chief Inspector. Margaret had a thing going with Foulis for a spell. We never met him but she could be talkative after a few drinks. It was the usual routine – hotel weekends when he was supposed to be working. Then it burned out.' He turned to his wife. 'How long ago?'

'A few months.' She touched her lips with her tongue. 'I don't know if it completely burned out. But somebody called Tulley began moving in.'

Thane nodded. 'Did it end because Foulis's wife found out?'

Gibb chuckled again. 'Do they ever? No, I'd say Margaret Barclay was the kind of woman who needed a change of man every so often.'

'I feel that way sometimes,' said Jane Gibb bleakly. 'Are we finished now?'

Thane nodded and let them lead the way back to the lounge. As they reached it, he stiffened. Hunched in a chair, large and sombre-faced, Chief Superintendent William Ilford usually let a warning go out before he came calling. Greeting him with a slight nod, the city C.I.D. boss glanced at the Gibbs as they passed but said nothing.

As soon as he'd delivered the couple to the uniformed man at the door Thane hurried back. Buddha Ilford was still sitting as he'd left him and gestured silently at another chair.

'I didn't know you were coming, sir,' said Thane warily, obeying.

'No.' Ilford thumbed towards the door. 'Who were they?'

'Friends of the woman. They say there's an address book missing.' Thane wondered what was coming.

'I see.' Ilford took out his aluminium-stemmed pipe, slowly removed a scrap of paper he'd been using as a stopper, and took a long time over getting the tobacco going with a match. Then he puffed for a moment, eyes apparently fixed on his navel in the habitual, contemplative mood which had won him his nickname. 'Moss told me you'd be here. I wanted to talk to you, away from any desk.'

'Sir?' Thane wished he'd look up, stop puffing that pipe, do anything except just sit there like . . .

Like Buddha.

At last the pipe left Ilford's mouth. Next instant the stem was a pointer, the words behind it a snarl.

'Do you believe in witchcraft?'

Startled, Thane gave a lop-sided grin. 'No, sir.'

'It's been defined as a web of fraud and folk medicine,' said Ilford softly. 'There was a time when Scotland was rotten with it – or with fear of it. Like to guess how many witchcraft executions are on record?'

Thane shook his head.

'Over four thousand in less than a hundred and fifty years.' Ilford sucked deeply on his pipe again. 'We topped the European league per head of population, made the Salem witch trials look like a sideshow. In fact, we were burning them right into the eighteenth century – the last was Jenny Horne, an old woman accused of turning her daughter into a horse so she could ride to a witches' sabbat.' He snorted angrily. 'Men, women, children – half of them probably confused or mentally retarded. You only had to shout "witch" and mass hysteria did the rest, with the Church urging them on from the background.'

'But there's no law against it now,' said Thane softly.

'No.' Ilford glared disapprovingly at the interruption. 'After Jenny Horne the witchcraft laws were repealed – which must have been the only time in history we weren't a long way ahead of England in civilized legislation.' The glare faded and became a bleak smile. 'There were still plenty of witches around, of course. And they were still killed every now and then – there's a case on record of a Sutherland farmer who was hanged because he murdered one with a spade. You know what his defence was? That she'd been in the form of a hare when he hit her.'

He fell silent again, brooding over his pipe. The faint sound of a passing aircraft penetrated the room and through the window Thane could see its jet trail in the sky. He turned his attention to Ilford again, positive that the C.I.D. chief was stalling. The question was why.

'Thane –' the bulky figure leaned forward – 'witchcraft never completely died away. Now it's on the upswing. Don't ask me why. Maybe it's because the TV programmes are so damned awful. What matters is I could show you reports from half a dozen country forces . . . all with a witchcraft theme from the Evil Eye onward. But not one of them with evidence that amounts to actual law-breaking.'

'This one could be different, sir,' said Thane quietly. 'There's a chance it was a coven-ordered killing.'

Face impassive, Ilford reached forward and tapped his pipe out against an ashtray.

'That's part of the reason why I'm here. Some people a lot more important than you or me are in a panic about this murder – and they don't all live in Monkswalk.' He saw Thane's question coming and shook his head. 'No, you're not getting names.'

'Why not, sir?' demanded Thane indignantly. 'If . . .'

'Don't argue,' barked Ilford, cutting him short. 'We

know they're not involved. Except –' he stopped, unusually reluctant – 'well, except maybe for one man. Someone who phoned me at home late last night. He said you'd already come looking for him.'

Bewildered now, Thane shook his head. 'It could only have been a door-to-door thing, sir. We've nothing else that would fit.'

Ilford shrugged. 'All I know is he's scared and I'm going to find out why, for personal reasons. Then –' he rose heavily to his feet – 'then, if he does know anything, you can have him.'

'Do I come with you?'

'No.' It came flatly. Ilford crossed the room and stared at the nearest painting with disgust. He spoke again without looking round, a new, personal note in his voice. 'Colin, when I was a youngster my kind of religion was the strict old Scottish variety with the Devil and hell as real as wearing a clean shirt on Sundays. That wasn't yesterday, but some of it sticks. I'd like to go in and stamp out the whole nest of them.'

'Sir?' Thane frowned at the broad back.

'Forget it.' Ilford turned. 'We've a murder case, nothing more. If people's private lives become exposed in the process and show up nasty, we don't judge them. Agreed?' He didn't want an answer. Reaching into one pocket, he pulled out an envelope. 'As usual, someone used me as a messenger boy. Dan Laurence sent this.'

Thane opened the envelope, glanced at the note inside, and nodded. It consisted of a name and an address and the terse comment, 'She feeds the dogs at noon.'

'Nothing important.' He tucked the note away, deciding it was no time to explain the delicate relationships within Laurence's family.

'Like I said, I'm just a bloody messenger boy.'

Wearily, Ilford glanced round the room again. 'Finished here?'

Thane nodded and followed his bear-like figure towards the door.

J. A. Raddock, L.D.S., R.F.P.S., operated his dental practice at an impressive stone villa in what was known as Old Monkswalk. There was extra prestige in being located in original Monkswalk as distinct from its newer extrusions. Exactly why was difficult to explain – Old Monkswalk was located in a hollow and constituted a winter fog-trap. In summer the drains had a distinctive smell.

Still, it was a good professional location. The villa had ivy, trees, and a broad expanse of lawn. Its front porch gave a choice of day, night and surgery bell-pushes and Thane obediently pushed the latter. After a moment the door was opened by a tall, thin, fair-haired girl in a white coat.

'I've an appointment with Mr Raddock.' He gave his name, saw a quick flicker of apprehension cross her pale, delicate face, and added easily, 'My wife telephoned last night. Did she speak to you?'

'Yes.' She moistened her lips slightly. 'Come in, please.'

He followed her through the carpeted hall to a desk. She picked up a new file-card and faced him again.

'Private patient or Health Service treatment, Mr Thane?' It came out like paying or charity.

'Health Service.'

'Of course.' Her voice didn't change but her glance swept from his shirt-cuffs to his shoes.

They finished the form-filling and he was left in a waiting room where one other patient, a middle-aged woman in a fur jacket, was already installed. The armchairs were comfortable, the magazines new, and after a single glance the woman ignored him.

A slim, dark-haired nurse looked in after a minute and collected her. He had time to smoke a cigarette before there was a murmur of voices in the hallway and he heard the front door close.

'Mr Thane . . .'

He followed the nurse through into a lavender-tiled surgery which smelled of a faintly perfumed disinfectant. Music was coming softly from a radio.

'Our new patient, eh?' Tall and in his thirties with jet-black hair, Jack Raddock had high cheekbones and a smile which showed teeth as white as his thigh-length coat. He didn't bother to glance at the file-card the nurse handed him. 'Or is this the back-door approach, Chief Inspector?'

Thane raised an eyebrow. 'Maybe both.'

'So at least I'll get paid for my time.' Raddock gestured towards the waiting chair. 'I wondered. One of my patients gets murdered, the papers say Chief Inspector Thane is in charge, and somebody called Thane pops up on my list. Two and two make four, that's what I told the girls this morning.'

Nodding, Thane settled in the chair and tried to place Raddock's face. He'd seen him somewhere, yet no particular memory attached to the features. The headrest was adjusted, a pedal squeaked, and suddenly he was angled under the lights.

'Let's have a look.' Raddock peered at his opened mouth, tapping a probe dulcimer style along the teeth. Thane winced as it found the trouble spot and a moment later Raddock stood back.

'Sylvia.' He waited till the nurse came over. She looked in her twenties and had a firm, full bust. 'Pre-molar upper left one has a hole like a mine shaft. A couple of others need fixing but we'll stay with the pre-molar. Dressing only this time.'

She turned away, laying out instruments. Humming to the music, Raddock picked up a long-needled hypodermic.

'This first. Wide – it's only Novocain.' The needle jabbed into Thane's gum and was withdrawn a second later. 'We'll let that cook, Chief Inspector. How did you link me with Margaret Barclay?'

'We found a card from you behind her door.' Thane felt his mouth numbing. 'How long had she been coming here?'

Raddock frowned, crossed to a small index cabinet, fingered its cards, then brought one back.

'Two years. On this last treatment she was having a few fillings.' He swung the drill over and began changing its head. 'If a patient doesn't show for an appointment my receptionist sends a reminder. If they still don't appear . . .' he shrugged. 'Well, she was a private patient. But that's one bill I won't try to collect.'

'How well did you know her?'

'Better than some.' Raddock rubbed a hand along his chin. 'In this game most patients are just walking mouths. But Margaret Barclay brightened things up. She had nice legs and a good figure. Like you, Sylvia, right?' He grinned round at the nurse and slapped her lightly on the backside. She took it coolly and went on mixing the dressing in a small container.

'And apart from her being a patient?' pressed Thane.

'Sometimes I saw her at parties.' Raddock sobered. 'Easy now, Chief Inspector. I don't go to bed with my patients. The pitch is that I'd like to do it, but that's the boundary line. I've too much to lose.'

'You knew she was a witch?'

'Uh-huh. But she couldn't cure toothache. Let's get to work.' The drill swung over, whined, and began carving. 'Hold it steady. This one's tricky.'

Tensed, the whine almost filling his head, Thane saw Raddock's face close to his own. The eyes and cheekbones were what mattered. But still his memory refused to come up with an answer.

'Stage one.' Raddock stopped the drill. 'Rinse. We're halfway there.'

Thane obeyed and drew a breath. 'You're fast.'

'I work best that way.' The man gave a white-toothed grin and patted the drill. 'This one's Swedish with an air-rotor bearing and a water-cooled head. Gives me three hundred thousand r.p.m., so don't jog my elbow.'

He moved in again and the drill whined for longer this time. A momentary stab of pain hit Thane, but Raddock kept on, frowning in concentration. Then, at last, he relaxed and switched off. The drill was pushed aside and he hummed once more while he packed the cavity with a white cement.

'Right,' he said at last. 'Finished.'

'Thanks.' Thane wiped his mouth with a tissue. 'When was she here last?'

'Margaret Barclay?' Raddock checked his record card again. 'A week past Monday, in the morning. When . . .'

'She was murdered that night.' Getting down from the chair, Thane faced him. 'Dentists get to see people in the raw. How was she when she was here?'

'Quiet, quieter than usual.' Raddock scowled thoughtfully. 'I got the feeling she was worried about something. But she didn't say anything out of the usual except . . .'

He stopped.

'Well?'

'Just something that didn't make much sense. I'd cracked some feeble joke about whether she'd cast any good spells lately – you could do that with her. She didn't laugh, just looked at me and said that at

least people were safe when they'd nothing to hide.'
He grimaced. 'Well, it didn't work out that way
for her.'

'No.' Thane nodded at the record card. 'I'd like that.
We're sure enough about identification, but . . .'

'I know. Dental records are fairly final.' Raddock
handed it over.

'Thanks.' Thane slipped the card into his pocket.
'She didn't say anything else?'

'Not that I remember.' Raddock opened the door.
'Don't eat on that side till tomorrow and next time I'll
remove the dressing and give you a permanent filling.
And – uh – good luck.'

Outside in the hallway the fair-haired receptionist
was waiting at her desk. She had a slip of paper in
her hand.

'An Inspector Moss telephoned and left a message
for you,' she said quickly, as if anxious to get the
matter over. 'He asked if you'd go to this address.'

'Thanks. And I need another appointment.' Thane
took the message slip and glanced at it. 'Where's
Graham Crescent?'

'On the other side of Monkswalk,' she answered
shortly, checking the surgery diary. 'Off Veldon Drive.'

He nodded, remembering the rendezvous with the
Panda car. 'Inspector Moss didn't say why?'

'No.' She handed him an appointment card. 'Just
that you were to go as soon as possible.'

Graham Crescent lay off the bottom end of Veldon
Drive and No. 10, a small chalet bungalow, already
had a C.I.D. car and another of the Panda patrol units
parked empty outside. Thane left the Austin behind
them and crunched up the short gravel path towards
the door with a sense of dull foreboding.

He'd been seen arriving. An unusually pale-faced D.C. Beech appeared on the porch as he reached it.

'Chief Superintendent Ilford has just left, sir,' said Beech awkwardly. 'He found him.'

'Found who?' asked Thane quietly.

'The suicide, sir.' Beech's young eyes showed a moment's surprise at the ignorance, then he flicked over a page in his notebook. 'Thomas Dallas, widower, retired engineer, aged sixty-four – that's about all I've got so far.'

Grim-faced, Thane followed him in. The uniformed Panda cop was standing gloomily in the hallway beside an opened door, another Millside D.C. was moving around in the room beyond.

In the middle of the room a thin, bald-headed man in a dark blue suit lay sprawled on his back on the carpet. Someone had spread a handkerchief over his face. There was an overturned chair beside him and a small table, still upright, held a single sheet of writing paper weighted down by a small, empty brown bottle.

A fly buzzed somewhere in the plainly furnished room as Thane read the note, the words in a neat, old-fashioned copperplate, the fountain pen beside it carefully re-capped.

'I renounce the Devil and all his works. May God help me. Thomas Dallas.'

He turned to Beech, his voice coming harsh. 'Was there anything else?'

Beech moistened his lips. 'There was another note pinned to the front door, telling the daily help to take the morning off. Chief Superintendent Ilford forced his way in, then called Division.' He glanced down. 'I'd say he's been dead a few hours, sir.'

'But he had himself a bonfire first,' mused the other D.C. standing at the fireplace.

Thane joined him, saw the thick black ash on the

otherwise empty hearth, ash carefully stirred and powdered till there was no chance of even the Scientific Branch salvaging its secrets.

'Here's something else you'd better see, sir,' said Beech soberly, pointing towards a framed photograph on the wall.

It was a snapshot enlargement of two kilted soldiers in World War Two uniforms. The proud hackle badge of the Black Watch was on their bonnets, they each wore corporal's stripes and were grinning at the camera.

One was a slimmer, younger Buddha Ilford. Mouth a tight line, Thane stared helplessly at the twisted body on the carpet. Thomas Dallas's claim on Ilford's friendship didn't have to be spelled out.

'Who have you contacted?' he asked absently.

'The local doctor knows him, sir. He's coming round.' Beech eyed him warily. 'Mr Ilford said to leave the rest till you came.'

'Relatives?'

'A son, but he's living in Canada.'

Thane didn't ask where the information had come from. Going over, he read the note again, then looked up bleakly.

'Dallas claimed we were at his house last night, looking for him. Know anything about it?'

The two detective constables shook their heads. Beech frowned. 'Nobody's been this way so far, sir. I've seen the list.'

'I know who it would be, sir.' The Panda constable had been listening at the doorway. He grinned awkwardly and came farther into the room. 'In fact, I would ha' been coming here myself sometime this morning.'

'Why?' asked Thane harshly.

'Motoring summonses, sir.' The Panda man patted

a bulging tunic pocket. 'My night oppo started delivering them last night.'

'Danny Seaforth?'

The man nodded. 'That's right. He left me a few for people who were out when he called. There's one for Dallas, careless driving an' going through a halt sign.' He sucked his lips uneasily. 'Hell, folk don't kill themselves over that kind o' thing.'

'He saw a uniform and a police car. With what he had on his mind that was enough,' said Thane bleakly. He turned to the two D.C.s. 'Go around the neighbours. I want an answer to just one question. Did they notice anything at all happening at this house the night Margaret Barclay was killed.'

They nodded and left. The Panda cop faded back into the hall again, deciding the background was the safest place on this one.

It was a small house, neat and tidy. Slowly, Thane went from room to room and saw Thomas Dallas had made his final preparations in fine detail. In the upstairs bedroom a neat bundle of documents lay on the dressing table, topped by the address of a city legal firm. Turning to leave, he heard a car drawing up outside, and when he glanced from the window a middle-aged stranger with a medical bag was leaving the driving seat of a small green Fiat.

The stranger was in the hall, talking to the Panda patrolman, when he came down.

'This is Dr Castle, sir,' introduced the Panda man. 'He was Dallas's G.P.'

Thane led the doctor into the front room. Unemotionally, Castle spent a few moments beside the body then crossed to the table and considered the small brown bottle.

'Barbiturates,' he said shortly. 'I prescribed them.'

'How many would he have left?' asked Thane.

'Enough.' Castle gave a weary shrug. 'He came to

me about a month ago and he should have been earlier. I diagnosed a combination of nervous tension and insomnia.'

'You've seen him since?'

'Once, a fortnight ago. I tried to find out what was worrying him, but . . .' Castle shook his head. 'All I could do was repeat the prescription. Even so, I wouldn't have figured on this. He wasn't the type.' He glanced at his watch. 'Your people will take care of the routine stuff, I suppose?'

Thane nodded. As the doctor left, Beech came back up the front path looking pleased with himself.

'We've got a start, sir,' he declared as soon as he'd entered. 'The neighbours say there were at least half a dozen cars parked outside this house that night, and none of them appeared till late on.'

'The coven meeting . . .' Thane said it softly, almost to himself. It slotted in absolute fashion with the rest. And if Margaret Barclay had been attacked afterwards . . . for once Beech was right. They had a start.

There was a telephone in the upstairs bedroom. He dialled Millside Division, with Beech hovering in a mild bewilderment at his elbow.

Phil Moss was out, on his way to take Frank Foulis to the mortuary and the formal identification session. But he got through to Detective Sergeant MacLeod, who sounded glum at being left holding the duty desk.

'I need a fingerprint team out here, Mac,' he ordered brusquely. 'I want a room by room search, every print they can collect. The ones I want will be old, but they may still be around.' Unless, he added mentally, Dallas's daily help worked harder than most. 'Then set up a detailed check on a dentist named Raddock plus anything you can get on two girls he has working for him.'

MacLeod carefully repeated the instructions. 'Where can I get back to you, sir?'

'You can't.' Thane patted his pockets, feeling for Dan Laurence's envelope and the address it contained. 'Tell D.I. Moss I've gone to meet a witch.'

'Yes, sir.' MacLeod remained unmoved. 'Whose side is she on?'

'Ours, I hope,' said Thane grimly. 'We need her.'

He hung up and found Beech looking at him wide-eyed.

'Something wrong?'

'No, sir.' Beech swallowed.

'Good.' Lips pursed, Thane gestured towards the front room. 'That photograph – I know someone who might want it later. But we might be doing that same someone a favour if it vanished for a spell.'

For once, Detective Constable Beech contented himself with a nod of surprising understanding.

Chapter Five

Loch Lomond was bright and blue and its islands were daubs of sun-splashed green. A few small cabin cruisers were moving on the water, pottering between the islands or maybe fishing for salmon. Visibility was good enough to pick out every detail of the houses on the slopes of the opposite shore though the great bulk of Ben Lomond and the other mountains beyond had their peaks hidden in white cloud.

Colin Thane kept the Austin at a steady pace along the narrow, winding A82 shore road, waiting for a chance to pass the massive cream-coloured tour coach just on ahead. He hung back far enough to stay clear of its stinking blue exhaust, part of his mind on the meeting ahead, the rest of it on a strange clicking noise coming from the Austin's engine area.

Almost certainly it was the water pump again. He cursed the unit and hoped it would at least last out till his next pay cheque. September was always the month when the bills came in like a postal snowstorm and the garage account was one he'd been hoping to trim.

The pump clicked on contemptuously. The coach ahead seemed determined to occupy the middle of the road, except when something equally heavy came from the opposite direction.

Bessie Roy, dog breeder and witch – or maybe it should be the other way round for all he knew – lived at Ossory Cottage, which was somewhere north of Tarbet village. He glanced at the speedometer, saw he'd done thirty miles since he'd left town, and reckoned another ten minutes should do it.

What he was going to ask her when he got there was another matter. So was whether she'd answer him. He lit another cigarette and grimaced at the belching exhaust ahead. Clay-doll curses, charms, and all the rest of the witchcraft trimmings might be just a fog obscuring what he should be tackling as a straightforward murder case. But now Thomas Dallas had killed himself. Through fear.

Whether the two deaths were separate or linked, he knew he had to learn at least a little about what he was up against.

And damn the water pump.

The tour coach pulled off the road at a hotel near Tarbet village. Thane fed the Austin a shade more accelerator and began to watch the signs at the verge, where rock and trees rose steeply leaving the road clinging to the water's edge. A rabbit streaked across the tarmac, pursued by something small and brown and even faster. Both disappeared from view in a death-chase along the shore.

When the sign came up it was a roughly lettered finger of wood which said Ossory and pointed to a narrow, partly concealed track to the left. He slowed the Austin, turned, and took the steep ascent in a bouncing low gear crawl. The track became a tunnel through a small forest of closely packed fir trees, and the car finally emerged on a gentle, grassy slope with an old grey stone-built house just ahead.

Beside the house, enclosed by a high chain-mesh fence, he saw a line of kennels. As the Austin neared them a miniature wave of dogs rushed towards the fence, barking and clawing at the chain mesh.

Switching off, he got out, grinned at the continued

93

din, and looked around. Ossory Cottage, a strange, circular-shaped building like an inverted cone, had a view down the whole long sweep of Loch Lomond. The trees screened the road as if it didn't exist, the hills to the rear were bare except for a few distant, grazing sheep.

Suddenly, above the barking, he heard a woman shouting. He turned, waiting while a tall figure in a plaid shirt and jeans came towards him from the kennels. She cuffed and shoved her way through the dogs, opened the compound gate, slammed it shut behind her, then walked over with a smile.

'Looking for me, Chief Inspector? I'm Bessie Roy.'

Thane swallowed. Bessie Roy was no crone with whiskers or any of the other possibilities Phil Moss had forecast. She was a slim, good-looking woman of about thirty, maybe less. Her long, black hair swung at her back in a single heavy plait and she had large, dark, faintly mocking eyes.

'Uncle Dan said you'd be coming.' Cool and confident, she tucked her thumbs into the waistband of her jeans. There was a man's watch on one wrist, a plain silver bracelet on the other. 'And he told me why.'

Behind them, the dogs' barking reached a new frenzy. Bessie Roy turned, shouted again without much effect, then beckoned Thane to follow her towards the house. The front door was open and she stopped him with a wave of her hand, whistling sharply.

The largest, ugliest-looking dog Thane had ever seen came padding out of the shadows in answer. As it saw him, its teeth bared and a growl began deep in its throat.

'Shut up, Archie. He's a friend.' Bessie Roy nodded encouragingly to Thane. 'Just ignore him.'

The growl died to a suspicious rumble. Thane eased

94

past the animal, following its owner into a neat, bright living room where there were flowers on a table and the walls were hung with glinting horse-brasses. There was a low, oak-beamed ceiling and a wood fire was smoking in the stone fireplace.

'Sit down,' invited Bessie Roy.

He did, taking one of the pair of rocking chairs beside the fire. Archie came over, sniffed his trouser legs carefully, then flopped down with a thud.

'He's – uh – big,' commented Thane.

'Irish wolfhound gone wrong.' Bessie Roy wrinkled her nose in cheerful disgust. 'He was a stray pup when I got him. Mainly I breed gundogs for the well-heeled gentry.' She sprawled down in the other rocking chair, considering him for a moment. 'Well, you didn't come here to talk dogs.'

'No.' Thane brought out his cigarettes. She shook her head as he offered the pack, but slid an ashtray across the polished wood floor. He lit his cigarette and said cautiously, 'Dan Laurence didn't tell me he was your uncle.'

'He doesn't tell many people I even exist.' She drew her long plait of black hair round from the back of her neck and rubbed the end between her fingertips. 'Having a witch in the family isn't the conventional idea of an asset. Maybe people don't burn us in tar barrels any more, but they make it pretty plain we're embarrassing to have around.'

Thane shrugged. 'I wouldn't know. I've got enough problems dealing with a mother-in-law.'

She laughed then grew more serious. 'Well, we'd better get a few things straight. I'm a "white" witch, Chief Inspector. That means I follow Wicca, the old faith, that I don't touch what's called black magic.' She gestured around. 'I've no cat, no cauldron, and I haven't used a broomstick since I was a kid and got a splinter where it really hurts. People like me believe

95

we're following a separate path to truth. Our powers are to help or heal.'

'What kind of powers?' asked Thane unemotionally.

'Sometimes to predict, though I can't make that happen to order. More often to use earth forces to cure friends or help them over problems. That sort of thing.'

'But you know about both sides?'

Bessie Roy flicked the plait of hair behind her again and nodded. 'I started off in a black coven. That was before I left school. Then I grew up a little, quit them, and I've been right-hand path ever since.' The dog began scratching and she dug a foot into its ribs. 'Archie, you've got fleas again. Sorry, Chief Inspector – the rest of the picture, if it interests you, is that I'm married to an airline captain. He's right-hand too. If either of us was left-hand, of course, we couldn't live here.'

'Meaning?'

'It's a round house.' She sighed at his ignorance. 'Any time you see an old round house in Scotland the man who built it was trying to cheat the Devil. He'd sold his soul, and promised to pay the debt at the gable end of the house. Except as there was no gable, the Devil couldn't collect – and no left-hand witch would live in a place the Devil disliked.'

He grinned, noting the portable TV set in one corner and the row of dog show trophies on a shelf. 'You believe that story?'

'Maybe not. But I'll bet the man who built this did.'

Something in her voice decided Thane it was time to move on. 'Bessie, I don't know how much Dan Laurence told you. But the best thing I can do is start at the beginning, missing out a few names.'

She listened quietly while he talked. A couple of times he saw her smiling strangely but there was no

96

other reaction till he'd finished. Then her mouth tightened.

'Margaret Barclay was a fool. She was short of money?'

He nodded.

'I thought so. No true witch can ask or accept payment for spells or charms. A gift is different, but even so . . .' She grimaced. 'I'd heard there was some kind of amateur coven in Monkswalk, with a left-hand bend, a black coven. White covens don't sacrifice blood – even a cockerel. We offer flowers, wine, things like that to the gods of fertility. About the only thing we have in common is that we dance naked at a ritual. Even then, we go clockwise and they go widdershins, anti-clockwise.'

She rose from the rocking chair, opened a cupboard, and brought out a whisky bottle and two glasses. Without asking him, she began pouring.

'Water with it?' she asked over her shoulder.

'A little.'

She added some from a jug and brought his drink over. It was a pale, fine single-malt and he sipped it appreciatively.

'Bessie, what kind of people would get involved in a black coven?'

'In a place like Monkswalk?' She settled in the chair again, rubbing her glass along one muscular thigh. 'One or two might be serious, the rest would be looking for kicks. We think of sex as partly a religious force. They wallow in it. As for meeting in the open –' she shuddered at the idea – 'when you're naked, central heating is a lot more civilized. If you want a guess, you're looking for a coven led by a warlock. Black covens are usually run that way – the fake variety. Some randy local decides he can cash in on the result.'

'But how much would they believe in it all?' he

persisted. 'For instance, if they decided to curse some-body, would they expect it to work?'

'Probably – and it might.' She looked at him soberly. 'Would you like it if you heard thirteen people had got together in a circle and ill-wished you?'

He shook his head. A belief in any kind of super-natural wasn't necessary on that one.

'Still, there are a few things that help,' she mused. 'A genuine black witch is scared of rowan leaves – most people know that one. Then there's the sign of Aradia, the moon goddess. That gives them the shakes.'

He thought of Seaforth and his rowan sprig, grinned slightly and waited.

'I can tell you about the ointment,' she said unex-pectedly. 'Margaret Barclay used it to fly. She must have been fairly advanced.'

He almost spluttered on his drink and stared at her. But she nodded seriously.

'It's true, Chief Inspector. That's the real basis for all the medieval stories about witches on broomsticks in the night sky. Except the witches concerned didn't use broomsticks or Fairy Caps or any of that "Horse and Hattock" nonsense.'

Suddenly he understood. 'You mean the flying was only in their minds?'

'You're coming on,' she congratulated with a faint sarcasm. 'They called it the Devil's Blessing. They took aconite and hemlock, deadly nightshade and other plant juices. Then they mixed them with fat – you could use margarine now, I suppose. The coven rubbed it on their naked bodies before they danced. Then, once they got going – well, their minds escaped from their bodies for a little while.'

Thane remembered how it had been and shifted uneasily in the rocking chair. It squeaked and the dog raised its head for a brief rumble.

'Shut up,' said Bessie Roy absent-mindedly. 'You've got me doing most of the talking, Chief Inspector. But go on – I don't mind. I'm not giving away any real secrets. And we've no love for black covens.'

He nodded then stubbed his cigarette slowly, thinking aloud. 'A witch could have enemies, Bessie. We know Margaret Barclay was worried, then she was "cut above the breath". Dallas, who was almost certainly in the same coven, was on the verge of a nervous breakdown. I'm talking about a motive for murder.'

She shrugged. 'There might be plenty. Once you get involved in witchcraft you've a simple choice – you stay quiet about it, as most do. Or you're open about it, and don't give a damn what people say. Most of us stay quiet, right- or left-hand path. To – well, to protect jobs or reputations or maybe families.'

Thane frowned. 'Margaret Barclay said something like that.'

'Then have you thought about blackmail?'

He hadn't before, but it suddenly made a lot of sense. 'Meaning she was squeezing the rest of the coven?'

'You're the detective,' she reminded dryly. 'But it might be pretty effective in a place like Monkswalk.'

'It would.' He could imagine the results, from panic onwards. 'Bessie . . .'

He stopped as a telephone began ringing. It was in an alcove just off the room. Getting up, Bessie Roy answered it, then turned, the receiver in her hand.

'It's for you.'

'Right.' Thane rose carefully to sidestep the dog, took the phone from her, and Phil Moss's voice greeted him.

'I got the number from Dan Laurence,' said Moss without preamble. He sounded more than usually aggrieved. 'How long before you'll be back?'

'I'm just about finished. Why?'

Moss grunted. 'Just that while you've been enlarging your education I've finished taking Frank Foulis's statement.'

'Well?' He glanced round, to find Bessie Roy watching with a concentrated interest. 'Any good?'

'It has more holes than my left sock,' came the acid reply. 'So what do we do about him?'

Thane thought quickly. 'Have you talked to Mrs Foulis yet?'

'No.'

'Then don't – and keep Foulis on ice till I get back. Where are you?'

'Still at the mortuary. It seemed a good place.'

'Get him over to Millside, Phil. I'll start back now.' He hung up and turned. Bessie Roy was still there.

'You've arrested someone?' she asked quietly.

He shook his head. 'But something's happened. I'll have to go.'

'Of course.' She came closer, the scent of the kennels coming faintly from her clothing. 'I wouldn't arrest anyone quickly, Chief Inspector. It might be a mistake.'

'Meaning?'

She shook her head. 'Call it a feeling I have. A feeling, nothing more.'

The dog padding at her heels, she went with him towards the house door. But as he reached it, she stopped.

'Please wait. I'll only be a moment.'

She hurried back the way they'd come, then almost immediately returned carrying a small cardboard box.

'Take this . . .' she began, then seemed to half-stumble over the dog. Grabbing Thane for support, she pulled herself upright, swore apologetically then put the box in his hand.

'That's for your friend, the one who telephoned.

Tell him to chew a little of what's in it any time his ulcer starts troubling.'

'What ulcer?' Thane tried to keep the surprise from his voice.

'The one Uncle Dan told me about when he phoned,' she said almost wearily. 'Will you?'

He nodded, muttered a thanks, and stuck the box in his pocket as she opened the door. The giant dog sitting beside her, Bessie Roy was still watching at the entrance to the round house as he turned the Austin and drove away.

Back on the main road, the water pump still clacking, Thane pushed his speed to the limit the other lochside traffic would allow. After a couple of miles, the traffic thinning, he relaxed a little and reached in his pocket for a cigarette. His fingers brushed Bessie Roy's cardboard box – then something else. Pulling it out blindly, he glanced down then swore softly, remembering how she'd fallen against him.

It was a small rowan-leaf shape, crudely cut from metal, sharp-edged, with a crescent moon hollowed from its centre. He guessed it was some kind of good-luck charm, grinned a little, and put it back.

Maybe Panda cops weren't the only people who should carry insurance.

Millside police station was unusually quiet when he got there. From the car crews washing down their vehicles in the parking lot to the men at the uniformed branch front office, everybody seemed to be waiting, knowing something was going to happen, uncertain exactly what it would be.

Upstairs, in the main C.I.D. room, it was pretty much the same. The small group of detective constables who'd been gossiping beside a window broke up quickly as Thane entered. One of them disappeared into the interview room and a moment later Phil Moss came out, closing the door firmly behind him.

'You made good time,' he said with a slight relief. 'Ready for Foulis?'

'As soon as I know what it's all about.' Thane propped himself against the nearest desk, frowning.

'That's easy enough.' Moss's thin face hardened. 'We went to the mortuary, he identified Margaret Barclay's body as if it was a lost bicycle, then I got my notebook out.'

'Voluntary statement?' asked Thane absently.

'No, I used thumbscrews,' said Moss sarcastically. 'Suitably cautioned and with Beech as a witness. Foulis says a couple of his party guests had too much booze in them to drive home. So he ferried them in his own car about midnight, when the party broke up. Then he says he had car trouble on the way back, took a while to fix it, and didn't get back home till about one-fifteen.'

'And that's all?' asked Thane grimly.

'Nearly. Except that he phoned his wife to tell her the car had broken down and that she can vouch for when he got back.'

'Weak.' Thane whistled thinly through his teeth for a moment. 'In fact, it's pathetic.'

Except that the weak and pathetic in alibis had a sad habit of remaining intact. He rubbed a thumbnail along his upper lip.

'The people he took home?'

'A couple called Herbach. They've confirmed their part. But they don't live far away, and there's still at least an hour unaccounted.'

Thane nodded slowly. 'And the car?'

'A Volvo station wagon – he says he had to clear a blocked fuel pump.' Moss sniffed deliberately. 'Traffic

Department sent over their engineering sergeant. He says that pump hasn't been touched in months.'

'Right.' Thane pushed away from the desk. 'How is he now?'

'Cool as they come.'

'Then we'll have to change that.'

The interview room wasn't much more than a cubicle with a frosted glass door, a table, and a few hard-backed chairs. Frank Foulis was sitting at the far side of the table, legs crossed beneath it, arms folded patiently.

Moss glanced at the detective constable in the background and thumbed towards the door. The man went out quietly, clicking the door shut behind him. Drawing a chair out from the table, Thane swung it round and settled in it saddle-fashion.

'I hear you had car trouble,' he began without preamble.

'It happens.' Frank Foulis's voice was cold, but his bearded face twitched slightly.

'To all of us,' agreed Thane. He rested his elbows on the chair-back and leaned forward. 'Clearing a fuel pump at midnight . . . no, it wouldn't be easy. Couldn't you get help?'

'At that hour?' Foulis unfolded his arms. 'The last time I called an all-night breakdown service they turned up two hours later. Anyway, I knew what to do, and I had the tools. There was some dirt in the pump filter. I cleaned it out, put the thing together again, and that was that.'

Thane glanced at Moss. 'Where did it happen?'

'He says Alban Street,' grunted Moss.

'I know it.' Thane nodded slightly. 'Residential and not much traffic.'

'None,' said Foulis coldly. 'Not when I was there.'

He straightened his tailored shoulders. 'Thane, I've been patient because I decided to stay that way the last time I was here. But what the hell is all this about?'

'We're hoping you'll tell us,' murmured Thane. 'You say you phoned your wife?'

'From a call-box. I didn't want her worrying.'

'I do that sometimes.' Thane smiled slightly. 'And she'll remember when you got home?'

'I said that already. It was about one-thirty and she was in bed, reading,' grated Foulis bitterly. 'Thane, I've had enough.'

'So have I.' Thane rose, came round to Foulis's side of the table, and put both hands on the scarred wood, just beside where some long-forgotten suspect had carved his initials. 'Foulis, I'm not interested in what you told your wife. I want the truth.'

Foulis stared up at him, opened his mouth, closed it again, and for the first time his eyes showed a trace of panic.

'What do you mean?' he managed after a moment.

Thane shrugged and deliberately turned away, nodding to Moss. Vary the voices, switch the approach, chip away for a spell. . . . Frank Foulis might have a business suit and clean fingernails. But the basic techniques didn't alter.

Moss grunted, staying where he was by the door, hands deep in his pockets.

'Like why you paid the rent for Margaret Barclay's studio,' he suggested laconically.

'So that's it?' Frank Foulis sighed and his bearded mouth shaped the faintest of grimaces. 'I paid for it, yes. And my wife doesn't know. Do I have to spell out why?'

Moss sniffed. 'Normally you could go fornicating around with anyone you wanted and it wouldn't be our affair. But we're talking about Margaret Barclay.'

'It still finished months ago,' declared Foulis harshly. 'It was when I'd hit a bad patch domestically and – well, that can happen, can't it?' He glanced appealingly at Thane. 'Everyone's human, agreed?'

Thane kept his expression wooden, stuck a cigarette in his mouth, and lit it without a word.

'Then there's the car,' said Moss unemotionally. He stopped, belched heavily, and went on as before. 'Foulis, a good liar always works on his story – even if it has to be afterwards. We've a police engineer who'll stand up in court and testify the fuel pump hasn't been touched. There's an unbroken layer of oil and muck over the whole unit.'

This time Foulis said nothing. He looked down at the table, moistening his lips, his face greying. Giving a brief hand signal to Moss, then sitting on the edge of the table beside the insurance chief, Thane took over again.

'Frank Foulis, you've already been formally cautioned.' He paused, giving Moss a chance to produce notebook and pencil, then went on with the same deliberate, cold formality. 'I remind you of the terms of that caution and that anything you say may be taken down in writing. Do you understand?'

Without looking up Foulis nodded.

'Then stop the bloody fairy-tales,' said Thane loudly and viciously. Grabbing Foulis by the shoulder, he forced the man round in the chair to face him, disgust in his voice. 'Do you know a man called Thomas Dallas?'

'No, I . . .'

'Dallas committed suicide this morning. Because he was frightened, because whoever killed Margaret Barclay lifted up a big flat stone that had been covering a load of crawling dirt.' Thane let go his grip, trying to keep control of his instincts. 'You took these people home. Then what really happened?'

Despite his size, Frank Foulis looked suddenly small. He hesitated, closed his eyes for a moment, then nodded. 'From the beginning?' he asked quietly.

'Yes. If it isn't another bundle like the last one.'

'It isn't.' Foulis sounded weary. 'But I meant it when I said I'd finished with Margaret Barclay. Just for a little while I'd thought . . .' He shrugged. 'That doesn't matter. I finished it, and she didn't seem to mind, even stayed friendly. She had the studio and a year's rent so . . .'

'You'd paid your bill?' suggested Thane grimly.

Foulis winced but nodded. 'She still came to the house, to see Kate. Carried it smoothly, too. I decided I could relax, that Kate wasn't ever going to find out.'

'You mean that mattered?' asked Thane stonily.

'It did.' Foulis chewed his lip. 'That's something you just have to believe, Thane. Because a couple of weeks ago Margaret suddenly began telephoning me at work, saying she had to see me alone.' He shook his head. 'I told her the answer was no.'

Moss gave a suspicious grunt. 'Did she say what she wanted?'

'I didn't give her the chance. I could guess – or I thought so.' Frank Foulis sighed and rubbed a hand over his beard. 'Then, God help me, Kate invited her to that damned party. She appeared with Tulley, bright as a button – except for when she got me alone for a moment. Then she gave me it straight. She'd done something which was going to land her in trouble if she didn't clear out first. She didn't say what was going on, just that I was going to give her a loan for old times' sake.'

The two Millside men exchanged a far from surprised glance.

'How much?' asked Thane.

'Five thousand or she'd tell Kate. But someone else came over and interrupted before she could say

106

more.' Foulis grimaced weakly. 'That's why I faked the car breakdown. I wanted to – hell, I don't know what I wanted to do. Anyway, I drove round to Chelor Grove, rang her bell at the main door, and got no reply. I guessed she was still out somewhere, so I waited in the car. A taxi came along about 1 a.m., but it was another woman who got out. That's when I decided I couldn't hang around waiting for ever. So I smoked another cigarette and drove home.' He looked at them in turn. 'Not much of a story, is it?'

'A jury wouldn't exactly weep for you,' said Moss cynically. 'Want to try again?'

Thane frowned him quiet. 'You say you didn't see Margaret Barclay?'

'No.' Foulis's voice was weary. 'Before you ask, I might have killed her myself that night – but I didn't.'

'The woman who got out of the taxi. Young or old?'

Foulis hesitated. 'Old, I think. She went into the apartment block.'

Thane considered him for several seconds, the stale smell of the interview room in his nostrils. Foulis's gloss was gone now. All that remained was a very worried man – worried and probably frightened. He made up his mind.

'You'll stay here. And we'll talk to your wife.'

'No –' Foulis scrambled to his feet – 'you can't!'

'You're wrong. And while we're doing it you'd better call your lawyer.'

With a noise like a sob Foulis went for him, hands clawing. A blow grazed Thane's cheek then he'd grabbed the man's wrists. For an instant Foulis strained against him, equal in height, surprisingly strong but not knowing what to do with it. Suddenly, Thane changed his grip and swung him round in a hammerlock.

'Don't be a damned fool,' he said almost mildly and dropped Foulis back down in his chair. Moss hadn't as much as stirred and he glared at him. 'Playing at statues or something?'

'You were doing all right.' Lazily, Moss opened the door and beckoned the detective constable back in.

Frank Foulis still sat slumped in the chair. On his way out, Thane stopped and looked back.

'We'll go easy on her,' he promised. But Foulis didn't look up.

'Believe him?' asked Moss as the C.I.D. duty car took them through the afternoon traffic towards Monkswalk.

'I'm not sure,' admitted Thane. He'd assigned Sergeant MacLeod to finding out when Mrs Polson had got back to Chelor Grove on the Monday night. Locating the taxi driver would take longer, but that was starting too. 'I'm not rushing it, Phil. One way or the other.'

He remembered whose advice that had been, reached into his pocket, and tossed Bessie Roy's cardboard box into Moss's lap.

'What's this?' Moss opened it, wrinkled his nose, and fingered the chopped, dried-up contents. 'Looks like string gone mouldy.'

'From Bessie Roy for you. She said chew some when your ulcer starts growling.'

Moss scowled and hesitated. 'Eh . . . any notion what it is? I mean, she's a witch. They've got funny ideas about things.'

'Shades of Macbeth?' Thane grinned despite himself. 'It could be old dog food.'

Cautiously, Moss took a fragment between finger and thumb and tasted. Then, more confidently, he tried a larger piece and chewed.

'Seems all right. Tastes like liquorice.' He tucked the box away, watching the scurry of pedestrians as they stopped at a traffic light. 'Was she handing out any-thing else?'

'Advice. Some of it helpful.' Thane suddenly leaned forward and tapped their driver on the shoulder. 'Ericson . . .'

'Sir?' Ericson glanced back warily through the driv-ing mirror, setting the car moving again as the light changed to green.

'What's that thing hanging from the ignition key?'

Ericson's neck reddened. 'Rabbit's foot, sir. I – uh – had it at home. It's just a notion.'

Thane sighed, remembered the metal clover leaf in his own pocket, and settled back again. Much more of it and things would start getting out of hand.

'Daft basket,' muttered Moss, still chewing. 'How lucky would you call an animal that ends being chopped up for ruddy key-fobs?' He turned back to Thane. 'At least your luck's holding, Colin. The Scien-tific squad say they've collected a barrow-load of fingerprints from the Dallas house, plenty of them different. They'll take some sorting out.'

'As long as we've got them, we've the start of a lead to the people in the coven.' Thane blessed the easy-going daily help who'd been lazy with her duster. 'And the background checks I wanted?'

'Should be on your desk when we get back. If they're still needed.'

Thane nodded. He'd need them, even if the Margaret Barclay murder was wrapped up. Partly because of Buddha Ilford. But mainly because a police uniform at the door had been enough to drive Thomas Dallas beyond fear and through terror to suicide.

An old story his father had loved to tell threaded into his mind. The one about the Free Kirk minister in a Highland glen who'd been lambasting his congrega-tion for their sinful ways. Yes, he thundered from the pulpit, there would be a 'day of reckoning, a time for a wailing and a universal gnashing of teeth.'

Which was when the minister had seen toothless Old Davie grinning bare-gummed from one of the front pews. And had quickly added:

'On that day, where necessary, teeth will be supplied by the Good Lord.'

Absently, he murmured the words aloud. Moss gave him a strange glance but he merely shook his head. It was something much more than a mildly funny story. It represented a stern discipline which had thankfully faded.

The trouble was that there was damn all left in its place.

Frank Foulis's home was a large white villa with green shutters, a dark Flemish tile roof, a double garage and Monkswalk's final status symbol, a discreet sign warning that the house was protected by night security alarms. The thinking behind it was you didn't bother having alarms fitted unless you had possessions really worth stealing.

The Millside car swung straight into the driveway and Ericson, democratic instincts roused, grinned as their tyres spattered gravel into the flower-beds. He stopped near the front door with a triumphant yank on the handbrake.

They left him there, Moss muttering a crudity about cowboys in uniform, and climbed the steps to the terrazzo porch. A middle-aged woman in a blue housekeeping overall answered the door and kept them waiting there while she disappeared back down the bright, polish-scented lobby.

Katherine Foulis came a moment later. The plump brunette wore a neat, plain blue two-piece suit with white piping on the jacket.

'Two of you for one small statement?' she asked with minimal warmth.

Thane looked at her, sensing a controlled antagonism behind the words. Plus something else less tangible but very different from the overweight butterfly image the same woman had projected before.

'We've been talking to your husband, Mrs Foulis,' he said quietly. 'He claims you can confirm some of his movements on the night Margaret Barclay was murdered.'

She stood very still for a moment then nodded her understanding.

'About how his car broke down on the way home?'

'Yes.'

'I see. Her lips tightened oddly. 'And do you believe that story?'

'No, Mrs Foulis.' He said it simply then wondered why he hadn't dodged behind one of the stock answers.

Surprisingly, she didn't flinch. Instead she almost smiled.

'Frank never was a very good liar, Chief Inspector. You'd better come in.'

Chapter Six

Frank Foulis and his wife lived well. It showed in the delicate Japanese water-colours hanging in the hall-way, then, as they were guided into one of the front rooms, in heavy velvet drapes, a display of Georgian silverware on a long sideboard and some of the thick-est carpeting they had ever crossed.

'Over here, I think.' Katherine Foulis carefully indi-cated a couch near the window, then took an armchair opposite. She sat down, smoothed her skirt carefully, and waited. Obediently, Thane and Moss settled side by side, feeling like two wise monkeys who'd mislaid a friend.

'The woman who answered the door . . .' Thane glanced in the direction of the hallway.

'Mrs Harrison, our daily. She goes after lunch – I saw her out the back door before I came through.' Katherine Foulis saw Moss glance at a used cup and saucer lying on a small table. 'There may be some coffee left.'

Thane shook his head. 'It's no kind of social call, Mrs Foulis.'

'I know that.' Her fingers stroked the smooth fabric of the chair. 'Is Frank under arrest?'

'No.'

'You mean not yet.' The round face showed a sud-den, pleading determination. 'Can I ask a favour?'

'We usually listen,' said Moss, shifting uneasily.

'Tell me how Frank said I could back his story.'

'That's not how it happens,' said Thane, smiling a fraction. 'You should know that much.'

'I do.' She nodded gravely. 'I also know Frank didn't meet Margaret Barclay that night.' Her fingers stroked the fabric again. 'But I did.'

They stared at her and she nodded.

'I mean it. What's more, I'll prove it. But only after you tell me what Frank said. There's a reason – a very important one to me.'

'Mrs Foulis . . .' Thane stopped, swallowed, saw the expression in her eyes, and changed his mind. 'All right. He said he telephoned home and told you about the breakdown.'

'That's right. Just after midnight.' She waited.

'Then –' he glanced at Moss, saw no help there, and went on – 'then he finally got back here about one-thirty and found you in bed, reading. But he admits the breakdown story was a fake.'

'Thank you. That wasn't what mattered.' There was an unexpected tremor in her voice, then the plump face was suddenly buried in her podgy hands and a muffled noise was coming from her lips.

Awkwardly, Moss got to his feet. 'Steady now . . .' he began. The muffled noise stopped obediently and she looked up, a trace of tears in her brown eyes. But there was no grief on her face.

'Men . . . two of you and you couldn't see what the damned fool was trying to do?' Katherine Foulis laughed, a short, not quite hysterical sound. 'He was trying to protect me. That's what Frank was trying to do, and that's all I wanted to know, all that really mattered. Because I wasn't here when he got back. I came in after he did.' She nodded vigorously. 'Yes, I mean it. And I played along with his story. I said I'd gone out in my own car to try and find him. Now do you understand?'

113

On his feet now, Colin Thane swore under his breath. 'You knew about your husband and Margaret Barclay?'

'Almost from the moment it started,' she agreed bluntly. Then, looking at them in turn, she added, 'I think I'd like a cigarette. And isn't it time someone cautioned me or something?'

Thane provided the cigarette and a light while Moss muttered a frowning way through the formal caution.

'Where do I start?' she asked as he finished. 'At the beginning?'

'It'll be easiest,' said Thane cautiously. Moss had gone back to the couch. He stayed on his feet by the fireplace.

'All right.' She took a quick draw on the cigarette. 'A friend told me about Margaret Barclay and Frank. But I'd already guessed and – well, I couldn't completely blame him. The reasons don't matter, do they?'

'Not right now,' said Thane softly. 'Go on.'

'We've no children, Chief Inspector. I was on my own and – well, I decided the sensible thing was to say nothing and do nothing. Just to hang on, hope, and – and sort out some personal problems I should have tackled a long time before. You understand?'

'I think so.' Thane saw Moss's slightly puzzled face but nodded.

'When a witch has your husband . . .' The laugh was humourless and cracked. 'It wasn't pleasant, Chief Inspector. Not when she still came round to visit. There was a time when I thought I'd go crazy – even began to wonder if she'd worked some kind of spell on Frank.'

'You knew when it finished?'

'I could tell.' Katherine Foulis stared at the cigarette's smouldering tip. 'We've been happier since then, happier than we've been in years. But very recently Frank began acting strangely, and I couldn't

114

be sure why.' She looked up. 'That's why I invited her to our party. I wanted to see them together. If it was happening again, I thought I'd know.'

They listened silently while she went on in the same level voice. How she'd watched through the evening of the party yet had still been uncertain when Margaret Barclay left. But when Frank Foulis telephoned home to say his car had broken down . . .

'I got out my own car,' she said quietly. 'First I went to Chelor Grove and saw Frank's car parked near a street light. I could see he was behind the wheel, waiting.' She smiled strangely. 'That meant he didn't know where she was. But I did.'

Moss cleared his throat determinedly. 'Why?'

'She left her coat and handbag in my bedroom while the party was on.' Katherine Foulis shrugged slightly. 'I looked through the handbag at the first chance. I – well, I thought I might find something to connect her with Frank again. There wasn't, but I checked a little pocket diary in it. She had two entries for Monday night, our party, then a scribble: "Graham Crescent, 11 p.m."'

'We haven't found the handbag. Or a diary.' Thane sucked his lips briefly. 'But we think there was a coven meeting at Graham Crescent.'

'That's what I guessed,' she agreed steadily. 'And I knew that afterwards she'd probably walk home along Veldon Drive – she liked walking at night. So I left my car out of sight and waited in a gateway.'

'For how long?'

'Quite a while, and it was cold.' The details came almost absently. 'But she did come at last, at about one-fifteen. I looked at my watch just before that, so I can be pretty sure. AND I knew what I was going to do.'

Rising from the chair, she went across the room and brought back a brown leather handbag from the

115

window-seat. Opening it, she began unwrapping a small bundle of paper tissues.

'I said I'd give you proof, Chief Inspector. When Margaret Barclay came down that road I stepped out of the gateway, told her to stay away from Frank and – and used this.'

Thane stared at what lay in the tissues. It was a safety-razor blade in a small plastic paint-scraping holder. A few dark flecks of dried blood were visible along the cutting edge.

'I slashed her across the forehead and she screamed.' The plump face winced at the memory, but there was no regret in her voice. 'If she'd lived there would have been a small scar, I suppose. But to her it would have meant something worse.'

'The cut above the breath.' Carefully, Thane took the blade and its tissue wrappings. 'Who told you about that?'

'She did, a long time ago – and I remembered.' Katherine Foulis drew a deep breath. 'That was all I did. She started to run away, and fell. I watched her get up, then I went back to my car and drove home. Frank was there ahead of me. He thought I believed his story, and I'm sure he believed mine. At least till yesterday, when we heard she was dead. Then . . .'

'Then he thought you'd killed her.'

'I think so.' Her brown eyes met his own steadily. 'Do you?'

'No.' He was sure of that, at least.

'That's always something.' She moved away, stubbed her cigarette in an ashtray, and smiled wryly at them. 'I didn't go mad or anything. At least, I don't think so. Though when I was going back to the car . . .' She stopped.

'Yes?'

'I thought I heard footsteps, as if there was some-one else around. I even thought I saw something

116

moving for a moment. But it must have been nerves.' She shrugged, restless now, and went over to the sideboard. Fingering some of the Georgian silver, she asked, 'When you take me to the police station can I see Frank?'

Moss was watching him, his thin face impassive. Staying silent for a moment, Thane wrapped the paint-scraper blade again and put it in his pocket while he thought.

Katherine Foulis's story wove into place with everything else they knew. It also let her husband off the hook. Just what they'd do about the rest of it . . .

He sighed. 'Mrs Foulis, we know where you'll be. Your husband should get here within the hour. We – we'll be back later. You understand?'

'Thank you.' It came with a simple acceptance.

'And another thing, Mrs Foulis,' said Moss, getting up. 'Your husband, he – well, he told us all about Margaret Barclay.' He paused uncomfortably, glancing at Thane for support. 'She'd started trying to put a squeeze on him for money. But you were right. The thing was finished between them.'

She didn't answer, but suddenly looked as if she was going to cry again.

They made their own way out.

Constable Ericson had a cigarette in his mouth and a girlie magazine on his lap when they boarded the car. He quickly stubbed the cigarette, shoved the magazine out of sight, then nodded towards the car radio.

'Chief Inspector Thane to report to headquarters in person,' he reported laconically. 'Nothing else for us, sir.'

'Be thankful,' said Thane dryly. 'Drive around for a spell. Anywhere – I don't mind.'

Ericson started the Jaguar and in a moment they were purring along the road.

'Poor bitch,' said Moss unexpectedly. Then, looking slightly shamefaced, he dug into Bessie Roy's box and began chewing. 'But she dumps us back at the beginning again.'

'Near enough.' Thane didn't feel too disconsolate. 'Phil, I've some work for you. Get hold of Tom Dallas's bank manager. I've a feeling you'll find he'd been drawing extra money recently – a lot of it.'

Moss raised a thoughtful eyebrow. 'More blackmail?'

He nodded. 'It has to be that. If Margaret Barclay was involved in it and the coven were beginning to realize who was squeezing them . . .'

'She'd want to get out, with as much as she could gather.' Moss chomped thoughtfully. 'All right, I'll buy that much. So it could have been someone from the coven who was coming after her when Mrs Foulis stepped in?'

'If we establish blackmail.' Thane glanced at his watch and saw it was already after 3 p.m. 'Once you've finished with the bank, head for Chelor Grove and pay a social call on our friend Mrs Polson. She'll probably feed you tea and biscuits.'

'Her again?' Moss was horrified.

'Tea and biscuits,' ordered Thane firmly. 'She's a one-woman switchboard on the local gossip network. Plug in and start her talking.'

Moss groaned. 'About what?'

'Just Monkswalk. Steer her from there.' He leaned forward. 'Ericson, are there any decent pubs around here?'

Ericson grinned but kept his eyes on the road. 'There's the Alpine Lodge, sir – it's pricey but I've been a couple of times. I know a blonde who works there.'

Thane nodded, deciding Ericson's private life might be more interesting than he'd expected. 'I'll meet you there, Phil. Say around five-thirty.'

'Who keeps the car?' asked Moss suspiciously.

'You can,' sighed Thane. 'Drop me at the next corner and I can catch a ruddy bus.'

Most bus drivers employed by Glasgow Corporation's city transport department would prefer to be Grand Prix aces. They handle their double-deck charges like Formula One cars and sing happy Irish rebel songs as they six-wheel drift round traffic islands. Unless they're busy mourning the horse that didn't win the two-thirty race.

The Monkswalk–City Centre bus Thane boarded was fitted with two-way radio, a bleak necessity which allowed the crew to call for help if late-night thugs started a riot. But as it screamed its way into the city the passengers seemed the people in most need of protection.

He got off thankfully in Saltmarket and sneaked into the headquarters canteen for a late-lunch sandwich and coffee. From there he headed across the street to the Central Division block where Chief Superintendent Ilford had his office.

The city C.I.D. chief's room was located at the far end of the ground floor corridor. Like every other caller, from the Chief Constable downward, Thane pressed the bell-push to one side of the door and waited. As the word 'enter' lit beside it he went in.

'You're late,' said Buddha Ilford, looking up bleakly from his desk. 'Sit down. I'll tell Dan Laurence and Doc Williams to come over.'

He picked up the internal telephone and began talking. Thane cleared a chair of newspapers, dragged it over, and placed it where the sun coming through

119

the windows wouldn't hit him straight between the eyes.

It was a shabby room, littered with files and ledgers. An old hand-grenade lay on the desk as a paperweight. Legend had it the windows had last been opened to clear the beer fumes the morning after World War One ended. Between the grime and the dust, any pollution expert would have demanded a breathing helmet.

But that was the way Buddha liked it, and, outwardly at any rate, he was his usual gritty self again. The receiver went down with a thud and he settled back, lighting his pipe.

'They're coming. While we're waiting, how about a progress report?'

'Yes, sir.' Thane kept the story tight except when Ilford rumbled for more facts. The pipe puffed away and the smoke haze grew thicker. Only a brief flicker of expression when Tom Dallas was mentioned broke the C.I.D. chief's wooden-faced concentration.

'Hardly one of your better efforts, is it?' he asked grimly as Thane finished. The pipe still between his teeth, he scowled at his desk, then slid a slim, clipped collection of typewritten sheets across. 'You've been waiting on these. I had them collected from your Division. Better look through them now.'

Nodding, Thane flicked through the report sheets. There were few surprises. Mrs Polson said she'd arrived home at Chelor Grove by taxi around 1 a.m. and had a vague memory of a car being parked nearby. More vague memories came from Dallas's neighbours. None of them could give any exact details of the cars that had arrived outside his home that Monday night. He went through the rest quickly, from copies of the formal statements made by Arthur Gibb and his wife to the rundown report on Jack Raddock. The dentist had a moneyed background and

120

the two girls on his staff both came from top-drawer Monkswalk families.

'No bright rays of light?' queried Ilford with minimal humour.

'No, sir.' Thane laid them down with a grimace, knowing how many patient, foot-slogging hours of work they represented for the Millside men who'd been involved. 'Except Mrs Polson does help confirm the Foulis situation.'

'Them?' Ilford chewed his pipe-stem resignedly. 'All right, I'll back you as far as the husband's concerned. Kick him home with a flea in his ear. Mrs Foulis –' he gave a heavy-shouldered shrug – 'we can't dodge that one, Colin. The charge is serious assault. But we won't oppose bail, and you know how it will go from there. First offender, good character, nervous strain and the rest of it – I'll bet on probation.'

'And publicity.'

'They'll survive. What matters now is where we go from there. The blackmail angle sounds likely.' Ilford removed the pipe from his mouth and made a deliberate job of examining the bowl. 'I didn't see Tom Dallas often. But I thought I knew him pretty well. If he could be fool enough to fall into this witchcraft slime then – well, anybody could. But I'll also say this. If he'd killed Margaret Barclay he'd have admitted it in his note.'

Thane nodded slowly. 'I didn't see him in that role. What I'm trying for is another lead into the coven – and I've at least one possible.'

'Good. You're still happy about this character Tulley?'

'If there was blackmail, he might have been part of the operation. But from outside the coven, maybe using Margaret Barclay.'

'And the Gibbs?' Ilford pointed the pipe towards

121

the report sheets. 'Their alibi isn't much – just that they were home in bed.'

'Most people are after midnight,' said Thane wryly. 'It's usually the ones still up we worry about.'

Ilford nodded then gave a grunt as the buzzer on his desk sounded. He pressed one of the answer buttons and straightened up as the door swung open.

Doc Williams and Dan Laurence came in together, the police surgeon still grinning at some private joke and the Scientific Bureau chief slightly flushed as if he'd been on the receiving end. Ilford greeted them, waved them into chairs and started off without preamble.

'You first, Doc – and keep it brief.'

'I'll do my best,' promised Doc Williams cheerfully. 'Mind you, I'm at a disadvantage. Broomsticks don't run in our family.'

Dan Laurence began a rumbling growl, but Ilford cut him short with a frown and glared at the police surgeon.

'Sorry.' Doc Williams looked anything but as he stuck his hands in his pockets. 'I haven't much anyway. The Dallas autopsy report will be straightforward suicide – drug overdose, contributory causes. Though he had an old wound in the stomach area. Wartime shrapnel, I'd say.'

Ilford nodded. 'Mortar bomb, Dunkirk.'

Doc Williams paused, frowned, but didn't comment. 'Right, you next, Colin. That witchcraft cream . . .'

'Flying ointment,' corrected Thane. He glanced at Laurence. 'Bessie helped quite a bit, Dan.'

'Good.' The Scientific Bureau chief said it glumly. 'I still wish I'd kept my mouth shut about her.'

'Flying ointment?' Doc Williams shrugged. 'All I know is what was in the stuff, and that's a mixture of drugs in the hyoscyamine group. Enough to kill off

122

half of Monkswalk. I'd like to know where she got hold of them.'

'Plant extracts?' queried Thane.

'Shoving roots through a juice press?' The police surgeon shook his head. 'No, I'm talking about manufactured drugs. At least, that's how it looks. The other thing I've done is check on some of the Monkswalk "cures" – or what the local doctors had to say about them.'

Thane glanced wryly at the report sheets. More of Margaret Barclay's patients were still turning up. So far they had twenty-two, covering everything from asthma to warts.

'The doctors weren't exactly happy about the competition,' mused Doc Williams. 'But they're agreed on one thing. The so-called cures came down to a mixture of folk remedies plus psychology, meaning these women believed in her – and that's half the battle.'

'No mysteries?' asked Ilford. He opened a drawer, took out a flick-knife souvenired from a Saturday-night gang fight, and began cleaning his pipe bowl. 'You're sure, Doc?'

'Well, in my experience . . .'

Dan Laurence sniffed and got a little of his own back. 'How the hell would you know? Most o' your patients come dead on a slab. They've damn all chance of answering back.'

'Very funny,' muttered Doc Williams. 'All right, what's your valuable contribution?'

'Hard fact.' Dan Laurence beamed and scratched his paunch. 'Those fingerprints from Dallas's place – we've isolated eight sets so far, including Margaret Barclay's, proof she was there that night.'

'Or sometime,' qualified Ilford cautiously.

'Sometime is good enough,' mused Thane. 'Any of the other prints on record, Dan?'

'None. But if you like to do some collecting . . .'

Laurence didn't bother to finish the offer. Gesturing towards his companion he became more serious. 'Doc sent me over that witchcraft kit o' Margaret Barclay's and my lads took it apart. There were some flakes of cannabis in the suitcase lining, so maybe this "flying ointment" wasn't the only stuff she used.'

'It's in pattern,' murmured Doc Williams. 'Still, there's no indication she had the suitcase with her at the meeting.'

'My guess is they'd something different from the usual rituals on the agenda. It was a worry night about blackmail,' said Thane. Reaching into his pocket, he brought out the tissue-wrapped holder and blade and passed them over. 'I'd like these tested, Doc. There's no rush, but the bloodstains should match Margaret Barclay's group.'

'Right, I'll see what I can do.' The police surgeon tucked them away. 'Anything else before I go?'

'Yes, in a way.' Eyes twinkling, Thane produced an envelope from the same pocket. 'Bessie Roy prescribed something for Phil's ulcer. Is it safe? I wouldn't want his guts to burn out.'

'Would he notice?' Doc Williams opened the envelope, took out the fragment of dark, stringy root and peered at it cynically. Then conscious of an amused audience he put it in his mouth and chewed carefully. After a moment his expression changed to one of surprise.

'I'll be damned!'

'Something wrong?' demanded Ilford sharply.

'No, it's liquorice root. Plain, ordinary liquorice root. But how the blazes did she know?'

'Know what?' asked Thane patiently.

'Well' – Williams looked around the smoke-filled room with an uncomfortable embarrassment – 'it's something pretty new the medical research labs are playing with. I read a B.M.A. paper on it not long ago.

124

Liquorice root contains a substance glycyrrhetinic acid, and the research bods say it's one of the best things around for gastric or duodenal treatment.' Taking the remains of the root from his mouth, he considered it sadly. 'Tell Phil . . .' He stopped and scowled. 'Damn it, somebody must have put her up to this!'

Dan Laurence gave a delighted guffaw. 'Well, it wasn't me. Like to borrow her spell-book, Doc? You might learn a few things.'

Even Ilford was grinning. Struggling for an answer, Doc Williams gave up as the telephone began ringing. Ilford answered it, grunted, and held the receiver towards Thane.

'For you.'

Thane took it. Sergeant MacLeod's voice sounded in his ear, cautiously concerned.

'I know who you're with, sir, so I'll keep it brief. We've – uh – lost Tulley.' MacLeod's voice was low, as if Buddha Ilford was sitting on his shoulder. 'Beech was tailing him by car and there was a traffic jam in the middle of town and . . .'

'It doesn't matter.' At least he hoped it didn't. Dan Laurence and Doc Williams were on their way out. Leaning back but obviously interested Ilford was lighting his pipe again. 'Tell Beech to come back in. And Mac, you can release Frank Foulis. Make sure he goes straight home.'

'Sir?' MacLeod was puzzled.

'Home,' emphasized Thane. 'Another thing, make sure we'll have a policewoman available this evening. Jean Cranston if possible.'

He hung up without further explanation, conscious he was really stretching the elastic leaving Katherine Foulis till then. But he had a feeling she wasn't likely to go anywhere.

125

'Anything interesting?' queried Buddha Ilford hopefully.

'No, sir.' Pushing back his chair, Thane decided it was time to leave. 'But maybe when I get back to Monkswalk . . .'

'Maybe is a word you're using rather a lot,' commented Ilford with a frosty edge. He glanced at his watch. 'Having any trouble from pressmen out there?'

'Not yet. They're around, but we're not tripping over them.' He wondered what was coming.

'Good.' Ilford disappeared behind a fresh puff of smoke. 'I've passed the word you'll hold a general press conference at 8 p.m. at Millside. Make the usual noises but tell them as little as possible, particularly about any coven theories.' He glanced at his watch again, manner losing some of its assurance. 'I've a telephone call booked to Canada. It should be coming through in a minute.'

'Dallas's son?' Thane didn't envy the C.I.D. chief the task. 'What will you tell him, sir?'

'That Tom was sick and –' Ilford grated, mouth tightening round the pipe-stem – 'and as little of the rest as I can.' He came forward on one elbow. 'Colin, from now on I'm going to try to keep out of this. Because if I came across any of this damned coven, man or woman, I . . .'

He didn't finish, a big, sadly angry man whose usual authority would count for nothing the next time that telephone rang.

The Alpine Lodge Hotel was a big, chalet-style building with a mock rustic finish, white stucco walls and a scatter of flashing neon signs. Colin Thane got there minutes after five-thirty, climbed out of the headquarters car which had given him a lift, then stood for a moment while the car swung away again.

126

Business seemed good at the Alpine Lodge. A long picture window gave a tempting view of a busy, softly lit cocktail lounge and the car-park area was already well filled. He couldn't spot the Millside Division car, but a chill gust of wind decided him against lingering.

Going in, he crossed the reception area and went through to the noise and bustle of the cocktail bar. Alpine murals covered the walls and the waitresses moving between the tables wore low-cut, mini-skirted versions of Swiss national costume. Then he spotted Phil Moss at a table near the bar and was halfway over before he realized Moss already had company. Drinks in front of them, Jane and Arthur Gibb greeted him easily as he took the remaining chair.

'I'm buying,' said the gaunt-faced agency man briskly. 'What'll it be?'

Moss had a beer in his hand. He settled for the same and Gibb gave the order to a passing waitress.

'Finding both of you like this is luck,' declared the man. He leaned nearer. 'Jane and I have a problem.'

She nodded and sipped her glass. 'We look in here once or twice a week on our way home. But if we hadn't spotted Inspector Moss we'd have been looking for you anyway.'

Staying silent, Moss gave him a faint, warning frown. He eyed the couple neutrally, waiting.

'The problem's called Drew Tulley,' said Gibb. He scowled and ran a hand over his thinning fair hair. 'Tulley turned up at our office this afternoon, wanting to weep on my shoulder. He says that even if you're finished with him there's someone following him around.'

'There was,' corrected Thane. 'We decided to keep an eye on him for a spell. But we've stopped now.'

'I told him it would be something like that,' said

Jane Gibb with a glint of cold amusement. 'Tulley's trouble is he's scared of his own shadow.'

Her husband grinned slightly. 'Then it's all right.' He stopped as the waitress returned with Thane's beer and paid for it with a flourish. As she went away, he added, 'He had some sort of notion he might be next to be killed.'

'Any reason why?'

'Like Jane says, he's scared. He thought the Monkswalk coven might be after him.' Gibb relaxed. 'Anyway, I thought I'd better tell you – just in case.'

'We'll soothe him down,' promised Moss.

Thane nodded but his attention had switched to the bar. Two new customers had arrived and were looking in his direction. Out of his white dentist's tunic Jack Raddock favoured casual wear. In a green sports coat and slacks and a roll-neck sweater, he waved a mild greeting. The girl at his side was his nurse, now in a tightly belted leather suit which made the most of her figure.

'Anything wrong, Chief Inspector?' asked Gibb.

'Just someone I know.' He turned his attention back to the table. 'Why would Tulley come to you?'

'Because he knew we were friends of Margaret's, I suppose. We'd met him a few times, and he needed to talk to someone.' Gibb drained his glass. 'Anyway, it looks like we can go home now. But any time we can help . . .'

'You can, one way,' said Thane grimly. 'You were at two coven meetings.'

'Where everyone wore masks,' reminded Jane Gibb wearily. 'We told you.'

'Even so, think about it. If you remember anything about the people who were there, anything at all, I want to know.'

'I know one of the women was blonde and had an

appendix scar,' chuckled Gibb. He grew more serious. 'All right, we'll try. We'll talk to Fred about it.'

'Fred?' Moss scowled uncertainly. 'Who's he?'

'A bear. Your boss knows him.' As his wife pushed back her chair Gibb followed suit. 'It's a family joke, Inspector. When we're talking about anything we use him as a sounding board.'

They left the table and headed out. Sighing, Moss looked at Thane for help.

'Forget it,' advised Thane. 'Where's our car?'

'Round the back. I gave Ericson a can of beer to keep him happy.' Moss's thin face brightened. 'Well, you were right about Tom Dallas's bank account. He'd been digging into it in a big way.'

'How much?'

'Enough for a blackmail payout. Two cash withdrawals, the first three months ago, the second last month, each for a thousand pounds.' He grinned a little at Thane's whistle. 'The bank manager said he was surprised too. But he's not paid to ask what people are going to do with money.'

'Except when it's overdraft time.' Thane glanced across at the bar. Raddock and the girl had moved to the window and were talking quietly, the girl frowning.

'We could have company in a moment,' he told Moss. 'How about Mrs Polson?'

'Once she gets going she takes some stopping. I've got the dirt on half the families in Monkswalk, including your dentist pal.'

'He's over at the window,' said Thane. 'The girl with him is his nurse.'

Moss grunted and looked across with interest. 'That'll be Sylvia Wishart – according to Mrs P. she does a lot more for him than sterilize the instruments. And he keeps his receptionist as a first-line reserve.'

'Sounds cosy,' agreed Thane dryly. Outside the window he could see the Gibbs driving away from the parking lot in their blue Alfa Romeo. 'Did she know anything about the coven, Phil?'

'Just whispers, no names – and she wasn't being coy.' Moss burped gently and tasted his beer again. 'Do you know how much they charge for a pint here?'

'More than I'd want to pay.' Thane grinned then murmured a warning. Raddock and the girl were heading towards them.

'How's the tooth, Chief Inspector?' asked Raddock heartily, shoving past a cluster of drinkers.

'No complaints,' said Thane thankfully.

'That's what we like to hear.' Raddock grinned round. 'Remember Sylvia?'

'She'd be hard to forget,' agreed Thane mildly.

'And she looks even better out of uniform, eh?' Raddock came closer and thumbed at the window. 'That's a nice Alfa Romeo your friends are driving. I know the man from somewhere. His name's Gibb, isn't it?'

'Yes.'

'Faces I forget, teeth I remember.' Raddock's grin broadened. 'I've told you before, Sylvia.'

'You've told me,' she agreed sulkily. 'Several times.'

Thane smiled dutifully, with a puzzle of his own every time he considered Raddock's flashing teeth and piercing eyes. The man's high-cheekboned face was beginning to haunt him, tantalizing his memory. Yet the reason kept eluding him.

'She gets bitchy when she's hungry,' declared Raddock, unconcerned. Bending nearer, he asked, 'Any progress on the case yet, Chief Inspector?'

'Let's say we're getting to know Monkswalk better,' said Thane dryly.

'That's an experience for anyone,' commented the girl with minimal interest. 'Jack . . .'

'Right.' Raddock winked a farewell and led her off.

Moss sighed, took a long gulp from his glass and finished his beer, then wiped the froth from his lips with one sleeve.

'He's cool,' he admitted. 'And dentists aren't my favourite people. Did our own people dig up anything on him?'

'A little.' It amounted to not much more than a few typewritten lines in the report sheet he'd collected from Ilford. 'Age thirty-eight, divorced, had a spell as an R.A.F. dental officer, drives a Jaguar, one conviction for drunk driving three years ago – nothing that matters much. Nothing on the girl except that her people are Monkswalk and have money. The receptionist is Iris Rother, same background.'

'Hand-picked.' Moss looked pointedly at his empty glass. 'Who's buying?'

'Me, but not here.' Thane flicked the tariff card on the table and shook his head. 'We'll go somewhere nearer home, where there's sawdust on the floor. Wait a second . . .'

Taking his handkerchief, glancing round to make sure he hadn't an audience, he quickly collected the used glasses left by the Gibbs. The glasses went into his pocket. Then, nodding, he got up and they headed for the door.

'Fingerprints?' queried Moss once they were outside.

'Yes.'

Moss looked puzzled. 'Any reason?'

'None I can spell out,' he admitted. 'If I'd had the chance I'd have grabbed Raddock's glass while I was at it.'

Moss took a fresh pinch of Bessie Roy's root from his pocket and began chewing. 'Let's get moving,' he suggested. 'Thieving isn't my strong point – I get nervous.'

The 8 p.m. press conference at Millside was no particular success. About twenty reporters crowded into the C.I.D. duty room and Thane knew most of them on first name terms. But that didn't help when they wanted facts and he was feeding back stock answers they could almost recite in unison.

At last their feelings crystallized in a groan from a lanky, long-haired stringer for a national Sunday. 'Let's try something easier, Chief Inspector. How do you feel about the weather?'

'The alleged weather,' muttered a voice from the background. 'And inquiries are continuing.'

'That's how it is,' admitted Thane wryly. 'Sorry.'

The conference broke up. He left Sergeant MacLeod the job of seeing none of the grumbling pressmen stayed behind and went back to his own room.

'Rough?' Slouched in a chair, Phil Moss had his feet up on the desk and a sleepy expression on his face.

'I've done better.' Thane closed the door with a sigh and lit a cigarette. 'Anything fresh?'

'Buddha Ilford wanting to know what's happening and calling back. Dan Laurence to say the Gibb fingerprints don't match any from Dallas's house. I asked him to give the Gibb prints a full run against main records.'

'Fine. And Mrs Foulis?'

'Being collected now, by a policewoman.'

The telephone rang before Thane could comment. Swearing under his breath, he guessed it was Ilford again and lifted the receiver.

'Thane.'

'Chief Inspector, it's Drew Tulley,' came the salesman's nervous voice. 'I – well, I'd like to see you. I'm at home. Could you come out, now?'

Thane sighed. 'If it's because someone was following you, forget it. He was one of my men.'

'No, not that.' Tulley's voice held a worried earnestness. 'It's something Margaret Barclay asked me about. I – well, it might matter, and if it does I want protection. Will you come?'

'We'll come. Just stay there.' Thane replaced the receiver thoughtfully.

'Where?' asked Moss, already on his feet.

'Tulley's place. And he sounds scared.'

'Good,' said Moss happily. 'That's when they start being useful.'

Drew Tulley's home was in a red-sandstone tenement block near King Street, close to Millside Division's boundary with Northern Division. It was old property in an area where the pubs saw fights most Saturday nights and building landlords didn't worry too much about repairs.

Fifteen minutes after Tulley's telephone call the Millside duty C.I.D. car stopped outside the tenement. The time included a brief delay while they'd collected D.C. Beech, who'd made the earlier visits.

'In there, Chief Inspector,' said Beech pointing to the nearest dim-lit entry. 'His place is two floors up. Want me to come?'

'Not yet,' said Thane, climbing out. 'But you're probably going to stay the night with him.'

'Sir?' Beech put a world of protest behind it.

'Think of the overtime, laddy,' consoled Moss, joining Thane at the kerb. 'And you can put a pie supper on expenses.

'Yes, sir.' Beech settled deeper in the car seat, cursing his luck. Another couple of minutes and he'd have been out of the police station and on his way home. Wednesday was his wife's bingo night, but she wouldn't have much chance now. When you'd a set of twins still at the nappy stage baby-sitters went into hiding.

But they never mentioned that kind of problem in the recruiting posters.

The tenement stairway was gas-lit, the steps worn at the edges, and the place smelled of stale cooking. Thane in the lead, Moss puffing a few steps behind, the two Millside men reached the second floor landing, saw Tulley's name on the nearest door, and rang the bell. There was a bright light shining above through a glass fanlight but no one came. Trying again, Thane held the button longer.

The light from the house went out and there was a strange metallic clatter from somewhere inside. Then silence.

'Tulley . . .' Moss thumped his fist on the door panels.

Pushing him aside, Thane tried the letter-box flap. Looking through the narrow slit, helped by the glow from the stairhead gas lamps, he saw a crumpled shape lying on the lobby floor.

Three steps back brought him to the banister rail. He charged forward, hitting the door with his shoulder. The lock collapsed, the door slammed back on its hinges, and he kept on going with it. Then, next instant, he was trying to alter direction as he glimpsed a shadow moving at the far end of the lobby.

Instead, he tripped over the limp figure on the floor and fell. As he landed, the acrid reek of paraffin hit his nostrils – and before he could rise a roaring blast of flame exploded from on ahead. Fierce heat and licking flame clawed an initial, roasting fury above him then formed a blazing, impenetrable barrier across the lobby.

Hair and clothes singed, the scorched air rasping at his lungs, Thane grabbed the limp figure beside him and started to drag it towards the door. Suddenly Moss was beside him and helping. Once they got their burden clear he rubbed his watering eyes and peered down.

It was Drew Tulley, his clothes smouldering, his face a bloodied mask, more blood oozing from his mouth.

Leaving them, Moss began hammering a warning at the nearest door while waves of smoke and a rising crackle of burning wood came from the apartment. As the first doors opened and the startled occupants emerged Beech and Ericson came pounding up the stairs, Ericson carrying the duty car's extinguisher.

Once the effort got under way it didn't take long. Using rugs, the extinguisher and buckets of water, minutes were enough to put out the blaze. But when they went through the charred hallway, past an over-turned paraffin heater with the tank cap unscrewed, and an emptied can lying beside it, the house was empty.

A back window lay open. Outside, a ten foot drop led to the top of a flat roof. Beyond the roof was a maze of huts and fences.

Whoever had attacked Drew Tulley, he was well away.

While his victim, pulse a mere flicker, lay with his grip on life fading. Someone had put an old bedmat under his head as a pillow. And it was already saturated with blood.

Chapter Seven

Colin Thane rode in the rear of the ambulance which took Drew Tulley through the night to the emergency casualty unit at the Western Infirmary. It was a big white Mercedes with an air-suspension system which made travel as smooth as a magic carpet while it cut a flashing, wailing priority path through the city traffic.

'We'll get him there,' murmured the ambulance attendant perched beside him. 'But I wouldn't take bets after that, Chief Inspector. Not the way he's been thumped around.'

They'd radioed ahead and the hospital was ready. As the ambulance pulled in at the casualty department door, two porters emerged with a trolley. Inside the hospital the night casualty officer, a young, pock-faced Pakistani doctor, gestured towards the nearest treatment cubicle, then followed the trolley and its motionless burden with a couple of nurses in his wake.

'Yours?' asked one of the porters when he emerged.

Thane nodded.

'There'll be some forms to fill and . . .' The man's voice faded as he saw the look on Thane's face. He shrugged and went off in search of the ambulance men.

Casualty admission was a long, antiseptic hall with

benches, anti-smoking posters on the walls and a framed request that patients refrain from spitting on the floor. Left waiting, wanting a cigarette but intimidated by the posters, Thane watched the steady trickle of patients who came and went.

Some sat quietly, resigned to delay, nursing minor injuries. A teenage ned left, his right ear newly stitched together again. As he went out, an elderly man arrived on a stretcher and was prioritied straight through to the cardiac unit. A child whimpered in a cubicle while her mother gave an hysterical explanation of how a kettle of boiling water had overbalanced.

After a few minutes the Pakistani casualty officer emerged from Tulley's cubicle. He shook his head at Thane's unspoken question, made a brief telephone call, then went back again. Another ambulance drew up outside and another stretcher was unloaded, a girl from a motorcycle accident. Her white-faced boyfriend walked beside the stretcher, holding her hand.

A new doctor, an older man with grey hair, entered the casualty hall from one of the corridors. He went into Tulley's cubicle and when he emerged again a nurse who was with him pointed in Thane's direction. He crossed over.

'Kendon, consultant surgeon,' he said shortly. 'I happened to be around on another job so now I'm landed with your man. He's pretty bad, Chief Inspector.'

'How are his chances?' asked Thane.

'We always try.' The surgeon looked past him, a scowl shaping as a staggering drunk was escorted in by a stony-faced Marine Division constable. The drunk looked as though he'd met the business end of a broken bottle. 'But God knows I get tired seeing our people stitching thugs together again – that wasn't what they trained for.'

'Tulley's not a ned,' said Thane patiently.

'Well, as I said, we'll try.' The surgeon glanced at his watch. 'He's going straight to theatre now. But anything I do will be just to try to keep him alive. If he does hang on he'll need major surgery later – though that's a pretty academic possibility.'

'Any hope he'll regain consciousness?'

'It's possible but not certain.' Kendon shook his head and refused to be committed. 'The head wounds look bad, but aren't my major worry. I'd say he was attacked with our old friend a blunt instrument then once he was knocked down someone gave him a thorough kicking. With murderous enough results – broken ribs, a perforated lung, and I'd bet on a ruptured liver.'

Thane chewed his lip. 'Internal haemorrhage, shock . . .'

'And the rest,' agreed the surgeon. 'If he dies, I'd rather it wasn't while I was working on him.'

'But we need his evidence,' said Thane quietly. 'If he does die then I've two murders – and no guarantee it will stop there.'

'We see murders every night. Except they're called road casualties.' Kendon turned at a squeak of wheels. Two porters were wheeling Tulley's trolley towards an elevator with a nurse in close attendance. The Pakistani casualty officer emerged unsmiling from the cubicle and headed for his next patient. 'All right, you've made your point, Chief Inspector. If you want my advice you'd better set things up for a dying declaration. Though I can't promise you'll even get that.'

The surgeon strode off.

Across the hall the drunk began calling the casualty

officer a black-faced bastard. The boy from the motor-cycle accident came back alone, weeping.

They found him a vacant office in the casualty hall, one with a telephone and a glass window which looked out on the reception area, and he began making a series of calls.

Buddha Ilford had to be first, then Division and the Scientific Bureau. Then Ilford called back to confirm that arrangements were under way. Finished, he was just laying down the receiver when Phil Moss entered the casualty hall, saw him through the window, and came into the room.

'I brought Beech and Ericson with me,' reported Moss, taking a chair. 'A squad from the night shift have taken over, and we found a hammer with bloodstains, but that's about it, Colin. None of the neighbours saw anything, heard anything, knows anything.'

Thane nodded absently, looked out at the casualty hall, saw Ericson and Beech arriving, and signalled them to wait.

'At that they were lucky,' he mused.

'Lucky?' Moss treated the word reverently. 'If we hadn't turned up the whole damned building could have burned down. What's the verdict on Tulley so far?'

'Bad.' He told Moss how bad and saw him wince.

'The hammer then a kicking? We're looking for a homicidal maniac.'

'If he's mad, he's cold-blooded clever with it.' Thane rubbed a tired hand across his chin. 'If the place had burned down as he intended, we wouldn't have had much to go on.'

'Not much of Tulley, that's for sure,' agreed Moss with an icy humour. 'So now we wait?'

Thane nodded, reached for a magazine, and began flicking the pages. But the print scarcely registered, his mind kept straying to the struggle going on to keep Tulley alive.

A lot depended on it.

Drew Tulley came out of the top-floor operating theatre shortly after 10 p.m. A young nurse with an Irish brogue brought them the news and simultaneously shepherded in the small, mild-mannered man who'd just arrived as a passenger in a headquarters car.

He looked serious and was about sixty. He wore a grey lounge suit, was bald, plump, and might have been anybody's favourite uncle. But his name was James Lewis, his working overalls were a judge's wig and gown, and he was a Sheriff-Substitute for the City of Glasgow.

They had fifteen minutes to talk before the nurse returned to guide them, via the elevator and a series of long, white-tiled corridors, to the entrance to one of the hospital's surgical wards.

After another couple of minutes the grey-haired surgeon emerged from a side-room. He raised an eyebrow as he saw Sheriff Lewis, smiled slightly but without explanation, then gestured towards the open door.

'He's conscious, but he hasn't got long and what you'll get out of him I won't guarantee. Sorry, Chief Inspector – medicine is still low on miracles.'

Sheriff Lewis cleared his throat. 'Does he know?'

'I told him,' said the surgeon bleakly. 'The rest is your job and you're welcome to it.'

Thane looked down at his feet. A dying deposition needed exact qualities to be valid under Scottish law. The person making it had to be a material witness

140

in a criminal case, his mind must be sufficiently clear to give reliable evidence, and he must be aware he was dying.

The legal doctrine behind it was centuries old. A dying declaration had to be made, said the textbooks, 'when every hope of this world is gone; when every motive of falsehood is silenced, and the mind is induced by the most powerful considerations to speak the truth . . .'

A dying man seldom lied. Or, at least, that was the theory.

'Let's start, then,' said Lewis resignedly.

They went in. There was a nurse by Tulley's bed-side, but she faded discreetly into the background, leaving him alone, a still figure with a head wrapped in a turban of bandages, face drained of colour, eye-lids closed and puffy, absolutely motionless.

Quietly, Lewis drew a chair up beside the bed and was careful to avoid the blood-drip stand and the tube which connected its plasma bottle to Tulley's arm. He sat down and leaned over.

'Mr Tulley . . .'

The eyes opened a fraction, then closed again. The faintest of sounds came from Tulley's lips.

'Mr Tulley, you've been badly hurt.' The sheriff paused. 'You understand me?'

'Yes.' It came like a whisper. Tulley's eyes stayed closed.

'The hospital people have done all they can,' said Lewis quietly. 'You understand that too?'

'Yes.'

'Do you hope to recover?' asked Lewis with a gentleness few people who'd ever seen him on a bench would have believed possible.

The faintest of headshakes was his answer. He drew a deep breath, glanced round at Thane, then went on.

141

'Mr Tulley, who attacked you?'

Drew Tulley's mouth twitched. He mumbled and gave a small, painful cough. Bending lower, Lewis frowned.

'Try, laddy,' he said softly.

'Man – no face. Could – couldn't see. Don't know.' The words slurred and ran into each other. 'I opened door – thought it was police.'

Lewis sighed and gave a fractional shrug.

'You wanted the police to come, Mr Tulley,' he reminded slowly and carefully. 'Why? What did you want to tell them?'

'Margaret.' There was a long pause and another cough after the murmured name. Then, just as Lewis was going to try again, Tulley's eyes forced open. 'Wanted to know. Asked me – asked me how to find out about cars. Car – numbers. Said it mattered. Said all – all done that way.'

'What was done?' asked Thane intently.

Lewis glared at him. For a moment Tulley's eyes peered around, as if seeking where the new voice had come from.

'Cars,' Tulley repeated feebly, his voice beginning to fade. He coughed again, a weak sound. 'She said it was cars. Who . . . who owned them.' The words became a barely distinct mutter. 'Wouldn't . . . wouldn't tell any more. Not . . .'

He started to cough again. Then his head lolled, the eyes closing. Grim-faced, Kendon moved forward, felt his pulse, and bent over him for a moment. Then he stepped back and shook his head at the nurse.

'Dead?' asked Sheriff Lewis mildly.

'No, but that's all you'll get,' replied the surgeon positively. 'Did it make any kind of sense?'

'I wouldn't know,' confessed Lewis. 'Ask Thane – it's his case.'

Both men looked at him.

'Yes,' said Thane slowly. 'I think it did.'

'Good.' Lewis turned away from the bed with ill-concealed relief. 'Usual time for golf on Sunday, Frank?'

The surgeon nodded and signalled the nurse to escort them out.

Beech and Ericson were drinking coffee with a nurse in the casualty hall's duty room. Moss fetched them out and it was raining as they boarded the C.I.D. car.

'Where to, sir?' asked Ericson once he was behind the wheel.

'That makes two of us,' murmured Moss. He elbowed Thane, frowning. 'What was all that car stuff Tulley muttered about?'

'The Gibbs – or that's the hunch I'm backing.' Thane nodded curtly at Ericson, who was still waiting. 'Monkswalk. You know where the Gibbs live.'

'Mind spelling it out for the peasants?' asked Moss petulantly as the Jaguar got under way.

'I'll try.' For a moment Thane stayed silent, watching while they swept down the hospital driveway. Glasgow University's main building was a massive black silhouette against the city's skyline glow. 'The Gibbs admitted they were at two coven meetings. Everyone was masked. They didn't know who was there – and the coven didn't know who they were. Right?'

Moss nodded. 'Well?'

'But what about the cars that were there, Phil? If the Gibbs noted the registration numbers then checked them out later . . .'

'How? Motor Taxation don't give that kind of information over the counter.'

'There's an easy enough way,' said Thane bitterly.

'Accept it was the Gibbs. They knew they'd seen the Monkswalk coven. All they'd have to do was look around the district – shops, the golf club, anywhere else cars pull in.'

'Spot one of the registration numbers, follow it home, then bang in a blackmail letter.' Moss whistled a soft understanding. 'Where it comes from nobody knows. Except that Margaret Barclay must have come around to guessing. All right, but can we prove it?'

Up front, Beech had turned in his seat and was waiting. Ericson kept his eyes on the wet, glinting road, but was equally interested.

'We can try,' said Thane. He'd been sorting it out, finding the pieces fitted. 'Remember how Katherine Foulis thought someone saw her that night? Suppose it was the Gibbs, that they heard about the coven meeting from Margaret Barclay and went to collect more car numbers. Suppose they saw her attacked and went after her.'

'To help?' mused Moss.

Thane shrugged. 'Maybe. Then maybe Margaret Barclay challenged them as the blackmailers. Or maybe it was straightforward. She was the only person who could ever link them to the coven – and the situation was tailor-made.'

Moss shook his head, not completely convinced. 'You can't be sure, Colin. There might have been somebody else we don't know about who could pull the same trick. Damn it, we wouldn't know the Gibbs existed if they hadn't sent that letter to her home. And it was posted after the murder.'

'So what's wrong with building an alibi?' Thane lit a cigarette and drew on it while the Jaguar's windscreen wipers ticked a sweeping rhythm. 'Including those little touches like a missing address book – if it ever existed. They had her keys, they could search her flat and be sure there was nothing lying around to

144

worry about. They must have been feeling pretty secure.'

'Till Tulley turned up on their doorstep this afternoon making worried noises?'

He nodded. Whatever Tulley had said it must have been enough to alarm the Gibbs. But they'd still played it cool and had made sure they reported his visit. While they were planning the next stage.

It had to be that way.

There were lights burning in the split-level bungalow in Ayer Crescent. Thane had the car stop short of the driveway entrance, left Ericson aboard with the engine running, then led Moss and Beech on foot through the pattering rain. The blue Alfa Romeo coupé was parked in the driveway and they could hear music coming from the house.

'Beech, get round to the back door. I don't want another disappearing trick.'

Nodding, Beech eased away into the night. They gave him a full minute then went on, and as they reached the coupé Moss felt the radiator grille.

'Still warm,' he reported softly. 'It's been out tonight, that's for sure.'

The porch gave shelter from the rain and the brightly lit hallway on the other side of the glass front door was empty. Thane pressed the bell and the three-note chimes rang loudly above the continuing music.

The chimes were answered in a way he hadn't expected. D.C. Beech came towards them down the hall and opened the door with an oddly apprehensive look on his young face.

'The back door was open, sir,' he explained quickly. 'What I've seen is a shambles. And there's no one here.'

They saw for themselves, room by room – where wardrobes had been tipped over, drawers emptied

145

and ornaments smashed. In the kitchen the food cup-
boards had had their contents scattered on the floor.
Entering the lounge, Thane switched off the radio
then swore aloud.

The giant teddy bear lay slumped like a corpse, its
head ripped from its shoulders and thrown to one
side, sawdust stuffing everywhere.

'It's like a bunch of savages passed through on the
rampage,' muttered Moss, joining him and looking
around with something approaching awe. He
frowned back at the door and raised his voice.
'Beech . . .'

'Kitchen, sir. Give me a moment,' came the shouted
reply. It was slightly more than that before Beech
appeared in the doorway. But he had a raincoat in his
hands with bloodstains spattered down its front and
on both sleeves.

'Where did you find it?' demanded Thane.

'In their washing machine, sir.'

The coat had the label 'A. Gibb' on its inside collar.
It smelled strongly of paraffin.

'Start trying the neighbours, Phil,' Thane said
bleakly and helplessly. 'Beech, get Ericson from the
car. Tell him to bring a torch and start looking around
outside. I'll phone Division from here.'

Moss grunted and they left.

The telephone was in a bedroom and still worked.
Thane dialled Millside Division, got through to the
C.I.D. duty room, and found himself speaking to
Hanson, one of the night-shift sergeants. Curtly, fighting down his feelings, he gave Hanson a brief rundown on what they'd found and told him to get more
men out.

'Yes, sir.' Hanson hesitated. 'But – well – if we still
want Gibb for the Tulley murder . . .'

'Just do it,' snarled Thane. 'Don't try to be clever at
the same time.'

He slammed the receiver down, leaving Hanson with an aching ear and an open mouth.

Slowly, Thane made his way through the bungalow and out the back. Ericson and Beech were moving around the garden, each with a torch, the beams of light catching the steady drizzle of rain. He watched them for a moment, seeing how the bungalow was shielded on either side by a thick laurel hedge. The same hedge ran along the bottom of the garden, but with a break halfway along.

Turning up his coat collar, the rain already trickling down his face, Thane walked down to the gap. There was a gate and it was half-open, on the other side a tarmac lane broad enough to take a car.

'Ericson.'

The driver trotted over, swung the torch around then steadied the beam as it settled on something lying just beyond the gate. Stooping, Thane picked up a thin metal necklet chain with a glazed pottery pendant. The chain had been broken. The pendant, handcraft painted, was a miniature devil mask.

Motionless, oblivious to the rain, the pendant cold against his hand, Colin Thane faced its reality. Arthur Gibb and his wife might be guilty of blackmail, murder, and more. But the Monkswalk coven had them, and he shuddered to think what that might mean.

He heard footsteps and turned. Moss trudged out of the darkness, a cigarette dangling from his lips.

'It happened half an hour ago,' said Moss laconically. 'At least, that's how it looks. The woman next door is waiting for her husband to come home from a Rotary thing. She heard a couple of cars drawing up then some noise afterwards. But she decided the Gibbs were having a drunken party and minded her own business.' He came nearer. 'What's that you've got?'

Thane showed him and Moss swore in sober detail.

'If that damned witchcraft mob have got them . . .' He paused, scowling. 'But how did they know it was the Gibbs they wanted?'

Staring at him, Thane didn't answer. The glow of Ericson's torch gave Moss's thin face a strange, saturnine outline for a moment. In that same moment something else clicked into place.

'Where's Beech?' he asked quietly, tucking the necklet in his pocket.

'Round at the front. One of the Panda cars had just arrived.'

He glanced at Ericson. 'Get Beech back to the car. Tell the Panda driver to keep an eye on things. If it's Seaforth and he's worried, better tell him he'll have company soon enough.'

Ericson grinned faintly and hurried off.

'We're leaving?' asked Moss, puzzled.

'Yes.'

'Mind telling me where?'

'Margaret Barclay's studio.'

Moss drew a deep, dangerous breath. 'And would it be too bloody much to ask why?'

'To try something,' said Thane. 'Wait till we get there.'

Moss glared, quivered, and belched his indignation at the night. Then, still scowling, he followed Thane back to the car.

It took only minutes to reach the lock-up garages near Chelor Grove. A small sports car was being driven into one of the lock-ups and its owner watched for a moment, curious, as they stopped outside Margaret Barclay's door.

'It'll be locked, sir,' reminded Ericson.

'Then open it,' said Thane impatiently.

Ericson shrugged, fetched a tyre lever from the

Jaguar's tool kit, and forced the lock in practised fashion. As he stood back Thane led the way in and switched on the lights.

'Over here, Phil.' Crossing the cold, stale-smelling studio, he went straight to the work-top and the pile of abandoned charcoal sketches. It was easy to find the few he wanted and spread them out.

'What about them?' asked Moss uncertainly.

'This.' Thane's finger stabbed down at the horned, grinning satyr on the serpent throne. 'And here and here.' His finger pointed to the same central figure in the other two confusions of witches and warlocks. 'The face, Phil. Who is he?'

Moss frowned, puzzled. Then his mouth dropped a fraction, and he peered closer, moving to each in turn.

'Jack Raddock?'

Thane nodded, his own last wisp of doubt vanishing, understanding now why the dentist's face had kept haunting him.

'He's the coven warlock, Phil. The man really running things.'

Moss leaned against the work-top, rested his head in his hands, and groaned. 'Then at the Alpine Lodge this evening, when he came over to us, he – damn it, he was really checking on the Gibbs!'

'On the Gibbs – and maybe seeing them with us clinched it,' agreed Thane softly, gathering up the drawings again.

'But why?' Moss licked his lips. 'Unless it was the car. The same trick in reverse.'

Thane nodded. The Gibbs had tracked down the coven by their cars. It would be a savage irony if the coven had used the same method. But there was no time to play guessing games. Rolling the drawings together, he put them under his arm.

'We'll try Raddock's place,' he said grimly. 'And let's hope we're not too late.'

Ericson had a message from Control waiting on them when they got back to the car.

Drew Tulley was dead. The cost of Monkswalk's folly was rising.

A church clock was striking eleven when the police car stopped just round the corner from Jack Raddock's villa. They could see its dark outline through the trees, but it showed no particular sign of life.

Another car went past, its tyres swishing over the wet tarmac. Then the road was empty and the night silent except for the gentle patter of rain on the Jaguar's roof.

'Take a look,' Thane told Beech. 'Don't fall over anything.'

Beech grinned, opened his door, and plodded off through the drizzle. Gradually, the car's windows began to steam up. Slouched behind the wheel, Ericson absently polished his tunic buttons with a sleeve and listened to the occasional murmur from the radio. But it was the kind of night when most of the city's neds seemed to be staying indoors, settling for beer and telly.

At last Beech reappeared. He flopped down into the front passenger seat, closed his door, and brushed the worst of the wet from his coat.

'It's getting bad out there,' he declared with a martyred air.

Moss grunted. 'Don't bother with the weather report.'

'No, sir.' Beech sighed and turned to Thane. 'I made a full circle of the house. No cars in the drive and the garage is empty, Chief Inspector. But there's a light in a room at the back and I saw someone moving inside. It looked like a woman.'

150

'Right.' Thane tried to keep the disappointment from his voice. 'We'll find out.'

The Jaguar purred to life, crawled forward, and swung into the villa's driveway. They left Ericson on radio watch, went to the front door, and rang the night bell. After a moment they heard footsteps then the porch light clicked on. The door opened a fraction, still held by a security chain.

'Yes?' Sylvia Wishart looked out through the gap. She recognized them and her eyes widened. 'What do you want?'

'A talk with Jack Raddock,' said Thane easily, the rolled sketches under his arm. 'Mind letting us in?'

The dental nurse hesitated, one hand brushing back her long dark hair. She'd changed into a button-to-the-neck shirt and old trousers, her feet were in a pair of scuffed moccasins. 'He – he's out. I don't know when he'll be back. I'm sorry.'

The door started to close. But Moss's shoe was firmly in the gap. 'You'll do instead,' he said smoothly.

Reluctantly, she loosened the chain. The door swung open and they went in.

'What do you want, anyway?' she demanded with open hostility.

'A talk, like we said.' Thane looked her up and down. 'Waiting on him?'

'That's my business.' She flushed then glared past him angrily. 'You – stop that, unless you've a search warrant.'

Moss, who had opened the nearest room door, grinned round. 'Have we one, Colin?'

'No. But we've this.' Thane took the devil-face pendant from his pocket and let it swing by the broken chain. 'Recognize it?'

She said nothing but her eyes flickered away from him.

'Check around, Phil,' said Thane quietly. 'Beech, tell

Ericson to call Control. Tell them I want a police-woman out here, fast.'

Beech nodded and went out, leaving the main door ajar. Shrugging, Sylvia Wishart led Thane along the hallway and into a small sitting room. A cigarette smouldered in an already well-filled ashtray and there was an empty glass beside it on the table.

'Sit down,' said Thane quietly.

'No. I'd rather . . .'

'Sit,' he barked.

Tight-lipped, the dental nurse obeyed. Again he held the pendant in front of her.

'I asked you if you recognized this.'

Ignoring it, she reached for the cigarette.

Thane got there first, deliberately stubbed the cigarette, then cleared the ashtray and her glass from the table.

'Take a look at these,' he invited grimly, spreading out the sketches. 'Margaret Barclay drew them. Recognize the face of that – that thing in the centre?'

Curiosity made her glance. Then the glance became a hypnotized stare. But she shook her head, her face a tight, hard mask.

'All right.' Thane left the sketches where they lay. 'Where's Raddock?'

'I told you. He went out. I don't know where – I'm not his keeper.'

'Just his mistress,' he queried mildly. 'Or is it your receptionist pal's turn tonight?'

Her fists clenched and she seemed ready to rise and hit him. Then, after a moment, she shrugged. 'Iris is at home. Check if you want.'

'Later.' Thane settled in the chair opposite and considered her coldly. 'About ten minutes ago a man named Drew Tulley died in hospital. Did you know him?'

152

Plainly bewildered, she swallowed and shook her head.

'Margaret Barclay did. That's why he was killed,' he said curtly. 'When we went to talk to Arthur Gibb and his wife about it –' he paused, seeing the gathering tension in her eyes – 'well, they were gone. Does that surprise you?'

'Should it?' she countered sulkily. 'I wouldn't know.'

Thane sighed and shrugged. 'Try again.'

He sat waiting, just watching, and a couple of minutes passed in absolute silence. Then Sylvia Wishart produced cigarettes and a lighter from her trouser pocket. Hands trembling a little, she lit one with a show of defiance.

'Haven't you anything better to do?' she demanded.

Thane smiled slightly, but shook his head.

She'd finished the cigarette before Phil Moss entered the room. Ignoring her, he turned to Thane.

'There's a playroom upstairs that would make you throw up,' he reported acidly, tossing a small leather-thonged whip on top of the sketches. 'Nice people.'

'Consenting is the word,' murmured Thane. 'Where's Beech?'

'Still looking around.' Moss glanced at the girl. 'Guess what we found in the kitchen. A nice, fat chunk of modelling clay. Made any good dolls lately?'

She licked her lips. 'We use clay in the practice, for – for dental moulds.'

'Complete with witchcraft pins?' Thane held her gaze. 'Look, we know Raddock runs the Monkswalk coven. We know the coven was being blackmailed and we know they've got the Gibbs. But understand this. Right now it doesn't matter what the Gibbs have done. If anything happens to them then the people involved, no matter how many, will have to pay for it.'

Though the High Court would probably have to build a bigger dock to hold them for the trial. He watched Sylvia Wishart again. Her resistance was fraying at the edges. But she still looked a long way off breaking point.

A car drew up outside. He heard the sound of its doors, then, after a moment, Beech escorted in the person he'd been waiting on. Policewoman Jean Cranston was out of uniform. She wore a neat tweed suit, high heels, and a tiny pillbox of a fur hat. Glancing at Sylvia Wishart, she smiled at Thane.

'Did you collect Mrs Foulis?' asked Thane absently.

'Collected her then brought her home again, sir,' she reported. 'Chief Superintendent Ilford's instructions – bail had been arranged and lodged.'

Thane raised an eyebrow, wondering how Ilford had managed that one. Then he came back to the present.

'Jean, I've a feeling that Miss Wishart isn't feeling too good. That she might even faint. But if her shirt collar was loosened . . .'

'It would help,' agreed Jean Cranston cheerfully. 'Will I find out?'

He nodded.

She went over, still smiling. Suddenly on her feet, Sylvia Wishart glared and backed away.

'Like to know why I'm here?' asked Jean Cranston in a voice that was still friendly. 'We call the reason "the two-second rape". Large male detectives don't like being left alone in awkward situations where a girl might start screaming. So I come along. That collar is too tight, isn't it?'

Suddenly, Sylvia Wishart clawed for her face. Sidestepping, the policewoman grabbed her arm, twisted, swore under her breath as the girl's foot clipped her ankle, but next minute held her securely.

'Finished?' she asked, tightening the hammerlock grip. 'Good.' With her free hand she unbuttoned the shirt collar. 'Sir?'

'See if there's a chain round her neck.'

There was. As she removed it, Sylvia Wishart tried to bite her wrist. Almost casually, Jean Cranston countered with a backhand slap across the jaw.

'Bitch,' snarled the girl.

Unperturbed, Jean Cranston let her go and brought the chain over. Another of the devil-face pendants hung from it, warm from the dental nurse's body.

'Why aren't you out with the rest of the coven?' asked Thane grimly.

Sylvia Wishart glared at him, all pretence vanished. 'That's my business. But I wanted to go, believe me.'

'She couldn't find her broomstick,' suggested Moss dryly, hands in his pockets. 'Hard luck.'

She gave a smile of cold contempt and deliberately smoothed her dark hair back in place. 'You're a fool, Inspector. There are many worse things than being a witch.'

'Even in a black coven?' murmured Thane. 'Most people would think differently.'

'Because they're blind.' Her voice was gradually taking on a fanatical edge. 'Black Donald gives us power. Power to smell out enemies, as we've done. Power to curse, to punish.' She took a deep breath, a frightening intensity in her eyes. 'You don't have to believe. Soon you'll have proof.'

'From the bunch you're with?' Thane shook his head sadly. 'They're playing at it, Hallowe'en games for kicks.'

'Some of them, perhaps.' Colour flared in her cheeks. 'But . . .'

'But not you?' Thane considered her thoughtfully,

155

knowing she meant every word, feeling strangely sorry for her – and for the way she'd handed him a possible weapon, one he had no option but to try.

Slowly, he unclipped the chain, removed the devil-face pendant, and felt in his pocket. Bringing out the little rowan-leaf charm, he threaded it to the chain through its crescent-moon centre.

'Ever heard of Bessie Roy?' he asked calmly. 'She's supposed to be fairly high up in the white witch league. Bessie gave me this – the rowan and the sign of Aradia, the moon goddess. She reckons they're both pretty powerful against black witches. What do you think?'

Sylvia Wishart moistened her lips. 'If you're trying to frighten me . . .'

'With a little thing like a good luck charm?' Thane laughed and came nearer. 'Try it on.'

'No.' She shrank back, her face paling.

'Why not?' Thane set the chain swinging like a pendulum. 'Did you know we've a load of finger-prints from the last coven meeting at Tom Dallas's house? We'll match them, Sylvia. One by one – if it means doing a door-to-door check through the whole of Monkswalk. Mind you, if we managed to get to the Gibbs before any real harm was done . . .'

He didn't finish, still coming nearer. She edged back, breathing quickly, a gathering terror in her eyes. Quietly, the pendulum swinging as effectively as any barrier, he forced the dental nurse into a corner of the room. A sound like a moan came from her lips.

'Sir.' Jean Cranston made a protesting noise, then fell silent as Moss's thin fingers gripped her arm.

'Try it on, Sylvia,' said Thane again. He brought the charm still nearer till it was almost brushing her breasts. 'Unless – well, unless you want to tell us where the Gibbs are now.'

Quivering, she didn't answer. Her eyes were glued

156

to the swinging chain, sweat was beading on her
forehead.

'Sylvia?' He let it touch her.

'At Harton Farm.' She pressed, almost shrivelled,
against the wall. 'It – it's a couple of miles from here.'

'I know it,' said Moss.

Thane stopped the swing. 'How many went with
them?'

'All the – the full initiates and some from outside.'
Now she'd started, it seemed to come easier. 'That –
that's why I'm not there. It – Jack said only full
initiates. I've still one level to achieve.'

'How many went?' he asked again.

'Maybe a dozen. I'm not sure.' She drew a deep,
shuddering breath. 'They – I think they're going to
kill the Gibbs at midnight. But that's all I know.'

'Midnight.' He glanced at his watch. They still had
half an hour but it wasn't much of a margin. 'How
did the coven know it was the Gibbs they wanted?'

'Because –' she moistened her lips again – 'because
of the last blackmail pick-up.'

'When was that?'

'The night after the coven meeting – after Margaret
Barclay was murdered. Some of us worked out a plan
to watch the money being collected. It was from a – a
roadside telephone booth. We couldn't get close
enough to see more than the car. But we saw it again
this evening and Jack knew who they were – they'd
been patients once.'

He exchanged a glance with Moss. Their guess had
been almost right.

Stepping back, he put the necklet in his pocket.
Sylvia Wishart staggered over to the nearest chair,
collapsed into it, and began weeping.

'Take her in, Jean,' said Thane quietly.

'Yes, sir.' Policewoman Cranston's expression said a
lot more.

'I know,' he agreed wearily. 'Call it psychiatric assault and battery if you want. She's sick in her mind and I haven't helped. But it worked – and right now that's all that matters.'

Turning on his heel, he walked out.

Chapter Eight

Fifteen minutes later he was crouching in a muddy ditch and peering through a gap in a low dry-stone wall. It had stopped raining and faint, clouded moonlight gave just enough visibility to let him see that the old farmhouse some eighty yards on was dilapidated and partly roofless. But the long barn beside it looked intact and it was from the barn that lights were flickering while a strange, muffled chanting reached his ears.

'Sounds like a celebration,' muttered Phil Moss, down beside him in the black shadow of the wall. Moss moved his feet and there was a faint squelching sound. 'As long as they keep that up there shouldn't be much else happening.'

Thane nodded, easing round to lean against the stonework. The car was about a quarter mile down the rough track which led from the main road to the farmhouse. They'd left Beech and Ericson there and had come on alone. But soon, if their luck held, they'd have ample reinforcements. Two car-loads of C.I.D. were on their way plus a patrol van loaded with uniformed men.

'How well do you know the place, Phil?' he asked in a murmur.

'From years back, when I was a kid and came out to help at the potato-picking.' Moss grimaced at the memory. 'Hard work and not much money. I heard

the family who owned it died out and some neigh-
bour bought the place for the extra land.'

'It doesn't look like anyone lives anywhere near,'
mused Thane. 'That bunch could kick up as much
noise as they wanted and nobody would hear it.' The
hands of his watch showed ten minutes remaining
before midnight, and he drew a breath. 'In we go,
then. But we're just exploring this trip.'

Moss nodded, feeling in his hip pocket for the
small, strictly non-regulation baton he kept there. The
top four inches of wood had been drilled hollow and
filled with lead.

'Don't worry,' he said acidly. 'I don't feel like being
witchbait.'

They rose, slipped over the wall, and moved
silently across the open ground towards the old farmhouse. As they reached it, the chanting from the barn
stopped briefly then began again.

'This bit used to be a garden,' muttered Moss.
'Masses of flowers and millions of bees in summer.
Got stung once, and . . .'

A nudge from Thane cut him short and they
pressed against the shadowed building. A solitary
figure had appeared near the barn. He strolled along,
the moonlight glinting on the double-barrelled shotgun cradled under his right arm. Pausing, he seemed
to look straight in their direction. Then a match
flared as he lit a cigarette. After a couple of puffs
he moved on again, disappearing from view beyond
the farmhouse.

'A friendly welcome extended to visitors,' said
Moss in a hoarse, relieved whisper. He rubbed the
smooth wood of the baton against his lapel. 'We could
take him.'

'Not yet. He might be missed.' Thane edged further
along the farmhouse wall, picking his way past some
broken glass from a smashed window. Reaching the

gable end, he glanced round then whistled under his breath.

The main farmyard lay beyond. Half a dozen cars were parked in its centre, one with its sidelights still burning. But the rest of the yard was far from empty. Like strange, black mechanical monsters a line of agricultural machines from a combine onward occupied most of the rest of the space with a couple of tractors at one end. In the background he saw a tall grain silo and several modern metal storage tanks. Harton Farm seemed to be used as an equipment and storage depot for the main farming unit.

But what mattered most was the new view they now had of the long barn. Halfway down the far side an open staircase led from ground level to a small upper door which looked like it would lead into a hay-loft.

He considered it for a moment, the strange chanting still forming the same muffled, eerie background. At his side, Moss had the same ideas.

'If we got up there and that door wasn't locked . . .'

'We'd have a grandstand view,' agreed Thane softly. 'But keep an eye open for the laddy with the shotgun.'

Moving swiftly, they quit the shelter of the farmhouse and worked their way across the yard. Then, with only open ground between them and the staircase, they hugged the shelter of a tractor and waited.

A full minute ticked past before the shotgun guard strolled round again. He passed close enough for them to hear his voice humming in tune with the sombre chanting from the barn.

The guard's footsteps died away. Easing out of cover, they saw him head towards the silo tower. As he vanished from sight again, Thane nodded and they hurried over to the staircase.

On tiptoe they climbed the open treads, reached the

door, and found it was held by a simple latch. It clicked open, the hinges creaked alarmingly – then they were through and had the door closed behind them.

The smell of hay was suddenly warm and strong in their nostrils. In a dull glow of light they saw it stacked roof-high in tight bales, each stack tied down by netting. The glow came from beyond and the chanting had grown louder.

Signalling again, Thane led the way. Dried stalks rustled against their clothing as they crept along. A louder rustle, and a rat scampered across their path then disappeared with a squeak of indignation.

Grimacing, Thane edged round another wall of bales, then stopped short and grabbed Moss's arm, holding him back in cover.

They were at the edge of the loft section, looking down into the expanse of the main barn. Below them, lit by a line of roof-suspended tube lights, was a scene which might have been one of Margaret Barclay's charcoal sketches brought to life.

Most of the barn was filled with bagged grain. But the centre area was clear and a nightmare circle of shuffling figures were performing a slow, anti-clockwise dance round a small farm trailer which had a tarpaulin draped over it like an altar cloth. In the middle of the circle, their hands lashed to a wheel of the trailer, Arthur Gibb and his wife squatted on the concrete floor in white-faced fear.

Stomach tightening, Thane stared down. Arthur Gibb's clothes were torn and blood matted his thinning hair. Beside him, eyes tightly closed as if trying to shut out what was around her, Jane Gibb looked on the verge of collapse.

There were a dozen people in the shuffling, widder-shins dance. The women were naked except for a short black velvet cape, the men had only a slightly longer, plainer version. Bodies already glinting with perspiration, all had carnival-style rubber masks which gave them grotesque animal features.

Subtly, the dance changed rhythm. The words of the chant altered too, but still made no sense, the language a relic from an old, demented past.

As it changed, another figure strode into the middle of the circle. Jack Raddock wore no mask. Clad from head to foot in a loose black robe, a knife in the girdle at his waist, a horned skull-cap firmly on his head, he took position beside the trailer. His eyes glinted as the chant grew louder, his hands spread in an obscene benediction.

Dry-mouthed, Thane stiffened as straw rustled. But it was Moss, edging closer to nudge him.

'Barn door. To your left.'

He looked. There, at least, was a solid enough reality. Two more of the coven were posted by the main door. Fully clothed but masked, each carried a sporting rifle.

For the moment he'd seen enough. Easing back, he signalled Moss and they retired silently into the gloom of the hay-loft. The chant became indistinct, the light faded. Then, as they reached the loft door again, Moss exploded in a hoarse, outraged whisper.

'They're animals. Worse than ruddy animals – and they're stoking up for something.'

Thane nodded, wondering how much of it was the dancing rhythm, how much of it might be due to drugs like Margaret Barclay's flying ointment. But the chanting circle were tightening to a deliriously emotional pitch. With the Gibbs waiting helplessly at the receiving end.

'How long till the other cars arrive?' he asked quietly.

Moss chewed his lip and frowned. 'Any minute,

163

if they found the road. But if they try a straight rush . . .'

It would be batons against bullets. They both knew it. Given time to unwind, to return to everyday sanity, the devil dancers below might be easy enough to handle. But they were approaching their climax – and they had the Gibbs, who had bled them by blackmail and had killed a witch from their coven.

There wasn't time for talking. Any more than there was time to get Buddha Ilford's sanction and draw weapons for some of the men who'd be arriving.

Ilford would sanction it, Thane had no doubt on that score. Unarmed police were still a basic of the Scottish system. But when individual need arose Ilford's creed was that no cop should ever have to take a bullet in the belly for the sake of tradition. Riot guns, small arms, CS grenades, body armour, and the rest were in readiness, stored at headquarters and at each divisional office.

Still, as far as Harton's farm was concerned, the whole collection might have been on the moon. He made up his mind.

'We'll remove the outside man first, Phil. Then I'll stay while you bring half the men we've got and feed them into the loft. The rest move the cars up and come straight in on signal.'

'What signal?'

'That shotgun we're collecting.'

Easing open the door, he checked that the farmyard was empty. Quickly and quietly they went back down the outside stairway and hurried across to the line of farm machinery.

'Here, Phil.'

Grinning, he paused while Moss gave a mutter of disgust and dutifully lay down on the muddy ground a few feet out from the nearest tractor. Then he crossed to the vehicle and crouched in its cover, waiting.

A minute passed. Twitching slightly, Moss made himself more comfortable and then remained still. The chanting from the barn was becoming faster, more fervent, and Thane felt his own tension rising at an equal rate.

Suddenly he saw a movement in the moonlight, hissed a warning to Moss, and crouched lower. The outside guard was strolling back from the direction of the storage tanks, shotgun still tucked under his arm.

The man was about twenty feet away when he saw Moss for the first time. He hesitated for a moment, and tightened his grip on the shotgun before he hurried over. As he reached Moss he stopped, looked round suspiciously, and carefully prodded with the weapon.

Face down, Moss didn't as much as quiver. The shotgun prodded again, then the man used one foot and tried to turn him over, peering down. It needed three strides for Thane to reach him and he was still drawing a startled breath, still trying to react and bring the gun round, when Thane's tightly clasped hands slammed a hammer-blow on the back of his neck.

He fell without a sound across Moss's legs. The shotgun thudded on the mud. Swearing softly, Moss struggled out from under him and tried to brush the dirt from his clothes.

'Phil . . .' Thane had the gun and had shoved their prisoner over on his back. The man wore a rubber mask with a pig's snout and bulging cheeks. As it ripped off, a young, pimpled face was exposed to the moonlight.

'The mask looks better,' growled Moss. He rolled the unconscious figure on its side and snapped on handcuffs, right wrist to left ankle. 'Gag?'

165

'Yes.' Thane turned to check the shotgun. It was a cheap twelve gauge, both barrels loaded with duck shot. He waited till Moss finished gagging the man, using his tie and a handkerchief, then helped drag him over into the shadow of the tractor.

As they reached it the chanting stopped. After a moment's silence a woman's voice screamed. Moss froze, staring at Thane. The scream came again.

'Move, Phil,' said Thane tautly. 'Everybody straight in.'

Moss swallowed, nodded, and sprinted off into the darkness. Taking a deep breath, Thane turned back towards the stairway. Before he opened the loft door he flicked the shotgun's safety catch to ready.

The screaming had stopped but he heard a mutter of voices as he reached the edge of the hay-loft and looked down into the main barn. The scene had changed. Arthur Gibb was still tied to the trailer wheel, but his wife was now spreadeagled on the platform, hands and feet lashed to its corners. Raddock stood over her, the rest of the coven clustered tightly around.

'Brethren.' Raddock's teeth flashed a smile of savage triumph as his voice rang out. 'Now we begin.'

A bay of delight came from his sweating, naked audience. Puzzled, Thane stared down from the straw bales while some of them dragged over a heavy wooden board and placed it squarely across Jane Gibb's body. She twisted and squirmed, her face contorted with fear, but was helpless to resist.

Raddock rapped a command. Obediently, the coven scattered briefly then formed a line. Suddenly, sickeningly, Thane realized their purpose. Each had a building brick. Prancing, shouting, they moved forward, laid the brick down on top of the board, then scampered to the end of the line to collect more. Even the guards at the door had quit their post and were taking part, their rifles abandoned.

Gradually the weight pressing down on Jane Gibb began to increase. As it would go on increasing, brick by brick until her body could no longer resist the pressure. Until . . .

The dark-haired woman understood too. A bubbling, wailing noise came from her lips. Gibb was struggling at the trailer wheel, straining against the ropes round his wrist, cursing and shouting.

Raddock's black-robed figure took a step towards the edge of the trailer. He sneered, bent down, and spat in Gibb's face.

The first layer of bricks covered the board. The beginning of the second layer was dropped into place by a fat, pendulously breasted woman with dyed blonde hair. Hands knuckle-white round the shotgun, Thane found himself praying for the sound of the Millside cars.

Then he stepped from cover. Pointing the shotgun over the frenzied heads, he pulled the trigger.

Like a thunderclap the harsh, flat blast echoed round the barn while the duck-shot pellets battered against the far wall in a full choke spread. The coven line stopped in their tracks and stared up, paralysed. Dropping on one knee, he sighted the remaining barrel on Raddock's chest.

'Stay still,' he shouted hoarsely. 'Try anything and you'll need a new warlock.'

First to recover, Raddock dropped a hand to the knife at his waist and bellowed an answer.

'Count us, Thane. How many could you stop – alone?'

'How many would try?' He kept the shotgun ready, wondering how long he could keep the clustered hate below under any kind of control. 'What about it?

Playing witches won't let you wriggle out of a life sentence, and it doesn't matter a damn who you are.'

The grotesque animal faces stared up at him in silence. A few were already beginning to edge nearer to the piled grain sacks which led like stepping stones to the start of the hay-loft. Thane licked his lips, wondering if he could really hear car engines in the distance. Then he glanced at the Gibbs. The woman seemed to have fainted. Her husband had collapsed against the trailer wheel, shaking with relief.

As if reading his mind, Raddock tried again. A long, gowned arm gestured.

'Coven brethren, this man and woman have been judged. We know their crimes. Black Donald's law . . .'

'Black Donald's backside,' jeered Thane loudly. 'We want them too, Raddock – for double murder and blackmail. All that interests your bunch of maniacs is silencing them, keeping their own social faces sweet and clean. That's finished. For all of you.'

A low moan came from the clustered witches. Some shuddered as if they'd been struck. But even so he sensed he'd played the wrong card, robbed them of their last hope. Slowly, they began pressing forward again – except for the two door-guards, conspicuous in their clothing, who started to ease in the other direction, to the outer fringe. From there, if they made a dive for those rifles . . .

'I said stay where you are,' he reminded bleakly, letting the blued metal of the shotgun travel a small, tight arc to underline his meaning. 'You tell them, Raddock. It's all over. Why should they build more trouble for themselves?'

The black-garbed figure didn't answer and the people below continued to edge forward.

Thane felt sweat beading on his forehead. In their present fever, control of the coven still obviously rested with their warlock. One word from Raddock and the whole crazed pack might come howling and clawing up the sloping grain sacks.

If they did, he had the shotgun and its remaining shell. His stomach tightened at the thought of the close-range carnage which would be certain. Yet if they came, if they reached him . . .

He moistened his lips again.

'Raddock?'

The man seemed to have been listening to something else. He looked up slowly, met Thane's face, and gave a bitter shrug of acceptance.

'Do as he says, brethren,' he ordered harshly.

They muttered sullenly. But they stopped.

Thane drew a deep breath and nodded. 'Right. Now take out that knife, Raddock. Cut Gibb loose – but stay where I can see what you're doing.'

Again Raddock seemed to listen to something. This time Thane heard it too, the sound of cars coming near and coming fast. But the others seemed oblivious.

'Whatever you want, Chief Inspector,' said Raddock tonelessly. Ignoring his audience's protests he drew the ceremonial knife from his girdle, stooped, and cut Arthur Gibb's bonds with a single angry slash. Freed from the wheel, Gibb collapsed on the floor.

'Drop the knife,' said Thane. He waited till it clattered on the trailer platform, the sound of the cars now like music to his ears. 'Now start moving those damned bricks.'

Raddock hesitated, then turned his head as the first car braked outside. The coven heard the sound too and suddenly understood. A woman screamed – and with a rumble of runner wheels the barn door began to slide open while more cars drew up and feet pounded across the farmyard.

169

Ericson and Beech were first through the gap. As a miniature tidal wave of uniformed men followed, the coven witches scattered in a squealing, scurrying panic. Only Raddock seemed unaffected. He stood where he was, fists clenched at his side, motionless amid the confusion.

As the din grew Thane found himself relegated for a moment to a near spectator role. He shouted a warning as a large man with a rabbit mask and a wobbling pink paunch made a pounding rush in the direction of the two rifles still leaning against the wall.

Ericson got there first. The police driver's baton arm rose and fell like a flail and the man crumpled with a howl of pain.

Still the shouts and screams echoed. Glancing round, Thane couldn't see Raddock. But Phil Moss was near the trailer, fighting off a scratching, biting woman who'd lost both cape and mask. Further over, a uniformed sergeant tripped, went down, grabbed a passing leg, and next instant was locked in a rolling, thrashing combat with another of the coven.

Suddenly two figures with flapping capes dashed away from the rest. In an instant both were scrambling up the sloping grain sacks towards the hay-loft and the one in the lead had a brick in his right hand.

Reversing his grip on the shotgun, Thane waited for them. Sweating, snarling, his mask hanging from one ear, the first arrived and swung at him with the brick.

Dodging, Thane almost sadly hit him in the stomach with the shotgun butt. Giving a single whoop of agony the man toppled backward and down to smash against his companion. Bouncing and rolling, they fell in a tangle to hit the barn floor beside a delighted

170

constable. He had them handcuffed together before they realized it.

Gradually, the noise and confusion was fading. Herded into lines along a wall, most of the Monks-walk witches now seemed to have lost all fight. Dazed, dull-eyed, a few pathetically trying to cover their nakedness, they still hardly grasped what had happened. The last fugitive, a screaming, cursing woman, was wrestling in the far corner with a couple of uniformed men.

Thane ignored her, still unable to spot Raddock's black-garbed figure. A group of his men were clustered round the farm trailer busy at the task of freeing Jane Gibb. But still no Raddock – and, he realized with a curse, no Arthur Gibb.

Scrambling down the sacks, he saw Beech leave the trailer and hurry out of the barn towards the cars. But the group of men were parting, eyeing him awkwardly as he came near.

'Colin . . .' Moss beckoned from the far side of the trailer, his thin face unusually grim.

Thane reached him and stopped, shutting his ears to the sound of the woman still screaming in the background. Jack Raddock was lying propped against a wheel, a hand pressed tight and high against his left side, blood oozing down the black robe and welling out between his fingers.

Moss pointed under the trailer. Tight-lipped, Thane bent down and knew no one had to worry about Arthur Gibb again. He lay on his back, his neck at a broken angle, blue eyes staring sightlessly at the knife which lay beside him in a pool of blood. Raddock's knife, the one he'd been made to drop after he cut Gibb loose.

'I saw it, sir,' volunteered a constable from the background. He was young, he'd lost his hat, and he had scratch marks down one cheek. Flushing, he went

171

on: 'This fellow under the trailer appeared with the knife and went for this other one. Then they – well, they went rolling out o' sight, sir. I tried to get over, but it was difficult.' He stopped and swallowed. 'I'm sorry, sir.'

Thane shrugged his understanding and glanced at Moss.

'Four stab wounds, all chest. Beech is radioing for an ambulance.' Moss shook his head slightly.

Raddock saw the signal. He stirred slightly and gave a mirthless grin. 'But not for me, eh? Still, we won.'

He coughed and blood bubbled on his lips. 'You can't change that, Thane. Black Donald's judgement . . . it happened.'

Nodding, Thane knelt beside him. A corner of his mind was shrieking that because he'd made Raddock cut Gibb loose one was now dead and the other dying.

'When you pull teeth for a living you need strong wrists.' Raddock forced a grin again. 'One twist . . . it was easy. The woman?'

Thane looked over his shoulder. They'd freed Jane Gibb and she was lying semi-conscious, moaning a little. Ericson was putting his jacket under her head as a pillow.

'She's alive,' he said shortly.

'Good,' said Raddock. He grimaced. 'She deserved to die. But this way it will be easier. For the rest, I mean.'

'Maybe,' answered Thane mechanically. 'Raddock, how many in the coven were being blackmailed?'

'Five . . . six counting Tom Dallas. They were being squeezed for . . . for every penny they had.' Raddock sank back against the wheel, coughing again, the blood trickling down his chin. The stain beneath his fingers was growing too. 'You knew they killed Margaret Barclay?'

'We came round to it.'

'And we guessed.' Raddock paused for a moment and seemed to gather strength. 'The whole coven heard Gibb confess to it. You . . . you've plenty of witnesses. We knocked them around a little. Then they talked. Said they'd . . . they'd give the money back if we let them go. Money? After what they did to us?' His face twisted. 'There was even a time when we suspected Margaret Barclay. She knew it, she was going to leave us because of it. I – I tried to tell you that once. Do you remember?'

Thane didn't answer. In the background the coven had become quiet, a few beginning to struggle into clothes brought over by one of their guards.

'Raddock, did the Gibbs say why they killed her?'

Breathing becoming laboured, Raddock nodded. 'She'd started asking too . . . too many questions. They didn't want to take risks.' He looked at Thane, eyes puzzled. 'Gibb said something about an ideal chance.'

'They had one,' agreed Thane softly.

'But we still found them.' Raddock's high-boned face creased with a mixture of pain and triumph. Then he coughed heavily. 'But you found us. How?'

'Sylvia.' Thane saw his disbelief and nodded. 'Eventually.'

'Sylvia.' Raddock muttered the name, struggling for breath. 'She'd have made a . . . a fine witch, with time.' He looked up with an effort. 'You still don't understand us, do you?'

Slowly, Thane shook his head.

Raddock laughed, a harsh, bitter, choked-off sound.

173

'Damn you all,' he said hoarsely.
And died.

When it arrived, the ambulance took Jane Gibb to hospital. The uniformed constable who went with her was also going to need treatment. His left wrist had been bitten almost to the bone. A few minutes later they started moving the prisoners, fifteen of them, cowed, partly clothed, most of them openly terrified of what lay ahead.

The mortuary wagon came last. It never had to hurry.

At Millside it was 3 a.m. before the last of the Monkswalk coven and their fellow witches were processed through the charge room. By then the cells were so full that a patrol van had to transfer some of the station's ordinary customers to temporary lodgings with Northern Division.

Doc Williams had been and gone, patching a variety of cuts and scratches on both sides.

When it was over, Phil Moss grinned happily, slipped some liquorice root in his mouth, and went up to find Thane standing at a window in the otherwise empty C.I.D. duty room. Thane didn't turn as he came over, still staring out at the glinting lights of the city.

Moss chewed thoughtfully for a moment, then stopped beside him.

'Do I say it for you?' he asked bluntly.

Thane shrugged and met his gaze reluctantly. 'Gibb and Raddock – I made a mess of it, Phil.'

'You've done better,' said Moss bluntly. 'You've also done worse. But you earned your keep.' He paused, mouth tightening. 'Anyway, who the hell gave you the right to presume you should be God-always perfect?'

For several seconds Thane didn't answer, looking at the thin, indignant face beside him. Then he nodded and gave a faint, wry grin.

'Nobody around here, that's for sure,' he agreed resignedly. 'All finished down there?'

'Finished, and it's quite a list.' Moss perched on a desk. 'One account executive, one justice of the peace, three company directors and wives, two students – do I go on?'

Thane shook his head. He reached into his pocket, brought out Bessie Roy's rowan charm, and let it dangle from its chain.

All finished? For a lot of people it was just starting. The first hospital report on Jane Gibb said she had a crushed pelvis. When she faced the court it would be in a wheelchair. It would be a long time before she walked again.

The coven? Inevitably, some would draw prison sentences. Probably a few would be lucky and be released on probation under the first offender code.

But other people would suffer too. People like Katherine Foulis and her husband. Like the families of the Monkswalk coven.

Monkswalk could condemn, ostracize and reject, no matter what other guilty secrets it might still be hiding. And do it viciously. Monkswalk had no time for losers.

Shoving the chain back in his pocket, Thane picked up his coat from a chair.

'Going home?' asked Moss, scratching casually under one armpit.

'Yes, might as well.'

'Any rush?'

'No.' Thane raised an eyebrow, curious. 'Why?'

Moss considered him solemnly. 'Remember that bottle of whisky Mary gave me last Christmas?'

Thane blinked. 'You mean you've still got it?'

'I was saving it.' Moss sounded defensive. 'Anyway, I never did like drinking alone.'

Go home at this hour and the dog would probably think he was a burglar anyway. Thane could also remember the bottle, a twenty-year-old single-malt.

'I'll always help a friend in need,' he declared fervently. 'Where is it?'

Moss gave a happy belch and led the way.